About the Author

John Peterson served in the Royal Air Force himself as a Ground Support Engineer. It was while doing this that he got the ideas to write *For Queen and Contraband*, his first crime fiction title. He knows the fictional events that take place in this book are all entirely possible.

John now lives quietly with his partner Sarah on the Wirral Peninsula in Merseyside or 'The Dark Side' of the River Mersey, as his friends and family call it, but he still visits Liverpool regularly to see friends and family. John was born in Liverpool in 1959, the eldest boy of five children. He has been lucky enough to travel the world during his lifetime, which has inspired him to write his crime fiction books.

He has now completed his second and third crime fiction titles, which are now both available at Amazon bookstore, his second book being *A Currency To Die For* and his third and latest crime fiction title *From A Jack To A King*. If you enjoyed reading *For Queen and Contraband*, check out his other crime fiction books.

For Queen and Contraband

John Raymond Peterson

For Queen and Contraband

Olympia Publishers
London

www.olympiapublishers.com
OLYMPIA PAPERBACK EDITION

A CIP catalogue record for this title is
available from the British Library.

ISBN: 978-1-80074-266-6

This is a work of fiction.
Names, characters, places and incidents originate from the writer's
imagination. Any resemblance to actual persons, living or dead, is
purely coincidental.

First Published in 2022

Olympia Publishers
Tallis House
2 Tallis Street
London
EC4Y 0AB

Printed in Great Britain

Dedication

I would like to dedicate this book to two important women in my life: My mum, Irene 'Rene' Peterson, and my old English teacher, Mrs Pritchard, from Gilmour County Primary School. Two women who had faith in me and gave me encouragement in life.

Chapter 1
The Divert

George had slightly dilating pupils and a layer of sweat on his neck and back, but it hadn't penetrated his white cotton shirt yet; he constantly shifted his position in his car seat.

Think cool calm and collected, he repeatedly told himself, "Keep cool," he said quietly under his breath. He sat in his car, in lane three waiting his turn to pass through the customs check. He'd just disembarked from the cross-channel ferry from Zeebrugge to Felixstowe and was awaiting a routine customs' check before being on his way. *"Good, no bloody dogs,"* he thought to himself.

It had been an uncomfortable four-hour crossing on the car ferry with some sea swells and uncomfortable seats that were not designed for sleeping or sitting on for over four hours. Nervousness combined with slight seasickness and nausea caused by the journey was what George was feeling now that he was back on dry land. He just wanted to clear customs quickly and to be on his way. The car in front of him had a kid aged about eleven or twelve who was kneeling on the back seat and mocking him by waving 'bye' through the rear window. This car was next and was waved through without any checks at all.

He was next in line with his Ford Mondeo, and on the back parcel shelf above the back seat was his Royal Air Force jacket and his air force flat cap with his RAF stripes and his insignia which was clearly on show. This was done deliberately as it normally ensured he was waved through customs with a friendly smile and usually without any checks. It didn't work on this occasion though, as the customs officer waved him into a holding bay for a stop and search. A thought instantly jumped into George's head: *"Haven't you seen the uniform, yet you prick or are you anti-military?"* His heart started to beat a little bit faster, but he showed no outward signs of being worried. He parked the vehicle in the checking bay, turned off the ignition and opened the driver's window.

"Morning Sergeant — Can you get out of your vehicle please?"

So, he had seen the uniform, this isn't going to bode well, George thought to himself. He tried to look as casual as possible when he answered, "Morning; I hope this isn't going to take long, Officer, as I only have a short leave, and as you can imagine, I'm itching to get home."

The customs officer shot George a stern look and said, "We'll try to get you on your way quickly then, sir," whilst thinking to himself, *"It takes as long as it bloody well takes!"*

After briefly searching inside the glove box and the car interior, he was satisfied that there was nothing of interest. He turned to George and said, "Can you open the boot for me now, sir?"

George did as he was told and opened the boot to reveal a blue standard regulation issue RAF holdall and an expensive-looking leather suitcase. The only other things in the boot were a small first aid kit and a red emergency triangle that was required to be carried by law in case of breakdown on the autobahns.

"If you can bring both your bag and the suitcase to the

table, please, sir, we'll soon have you on your way."

George grabbed both items from the boot, carried them the short distance to the table and placed them on the table as instructed all the time whilst trying to look normal. His heart was racing. The customs officer clicked open the suitcase latches but before opening it, he asked, "Did you pack these bags yourself, sir?"

George's heart felt like it was going to explode and at that moment he thought to himself, *Do you think I had my valet pack them for me, you idiot?"* but instead, he found himself saying, "Yes I did, and can you stop calling me 'sir'! I work for a living, is all this absolutely necessary? I do have a long way to go before I can start my leave."

The customs officer did not reply; instead, he opened the leather suitcase first and this contained George's clothes, shoes and toiletries—nothing unusual. He then moved on to the blue RAF bag and unzipped it. In it, under some strategically placed items of light clothing, he discovered six boxes of King Edward cigars which contained fifty cigars in each box.

The officer's response was instant, "You know that you should have declared these, sir! You're only allowed one box, and I'm sure you already know this, as it's not your first time through customs, is it?"

George looked at him apologetically. "Yes, I'm sorry they are for my dad; he gets through them at an unbelievable rate. Can you possibly turn a blind eye? Just this once!"

The customs officer showed no emotion as he said, "I'm afraid I am going to have to confiscate five boxes and I have got to give you an official warning, Sergeant." It was the second time he had addressed George using his rank, so he had seen the uniform on the parcel shelf, and military! *Just my luck,* George thought to himself.

George took a deep breath and said, "Look, Officer, it's only a few cigars. You know what my job is if there is a nuclear war?"

The customs officer just looked at him with a blank expression.

George continued, "During a war, we have red channels and green channels on military bases to sort out who is allowed on to the bases and to take refuge in the nuclear bunkers. It's men like me who decide who we let in and who goes in the red channels. I would put you in the green channel, Officer." George wondered if he was overdoing the sucking-up. He continued anyway, "If you give me a warning that might get back to my superiors and could affect my military career, all for a few cigars, you wouldn't want that now, would you?"

The customs officer smiled and said sarcastically, "I'm still going to have to confiscate the five boxes irrespective of what channel you would put me in — but you can pack the rest of your gear and be on your way. Have a happy leave but don't try this again, or your channel story won't work next time, do you understand me, Sergeant?"

George said, "Thanks I understand, and it's much appreciated."

He quickly repacked his things and put the suitcase and his RAF bag minus the five boxes of cigars back into his car boot. He got back into his car and drove out of the customs building and out of Felixstowe Port. He got on to the A14 dual carriageway, which leads to the motorway and home. Flight Sergeant George Stewart thought to himself, *"It's certainly going to be a very happy leave now, Officer, you idiot!"* Before joining the motorway George stopped briefly to make a quick phone call from a public telephone box. A voice at the other end of the line answered, "Hello, Squadron Leader Walker

RAF Brüggen?"

George just said, "I'm through, no problems, all went exactly as planned," and replaced the telephone receiver.

The cigar decoy had worked exactly as they had planned: he was stopped, and the cigars were supposed to be found. Also in the car, hidden under the back seat of the Ford Mondeo was ten kilos of the finest Colombian cocaine, which has been double vacuum packed to prevent detection from customs sniffer dogs. A simple diversion technique, that'd worked perfectly.

Chapter 2
The Organisation

It took George the best part of another five hours to drive from Felixstowe to Liverpool. He'd stopped only once during the journey home at a motorway service station to fill up with petrol and to get a cup of coffee and something that didn't look very edible. Whilst eating his plate of macaroni and cheese, he thought to himself that the UK motorway service stations were probably the worst places to eat in the whole country and he was right.

It was getting dark as he retrieved a remote control from the small compartment located on the right side of his car dashboard. He pressed a button and his driveway gates slowly started to open. The gates led up a small solar-lit driveway to his smart detached house located in the pretty little village of Hale, on the outskirts of Liverpool. He drove through the gates and up the short driveway towards his detached house. The fading light just allowed him to notice how smart the garden was looking. George had an arrangement with a local friend, who was also a handyman who would carry out maintenance work on his house and gardens once a week. This ensured that his house and gardens were kept in pristine condition whilst he was away in the RAF. George liked everything to be neat and tidy, which was a trait he had embraced whilst in the RAF. He stopped the car at the end of the drive and entered his house alarm code on the same remote control to deactivate it. He then pressed a button on his key fob to open the electric roller shutter garage door. George liked technology and his labour-saving gadgets, another facet of his personality that he'd picked up from his time in the services. As he drove into the garage through the roller shutter door, the movement of his car activated sensors which automatically switched on the garage lights, illuminating the garage. In the left-hand parking bay there was another vehicle that was covered by a snugly fitting lightweight cover and underneath the cover was his pride and joy. He carefully parked his two-year-old Ford Mondeo in the bay and pressed the button on his fob to close the garage door. He got out of his car and could hardly contain himself as he gently removed the cover on the other car and revealed a stunning cobalt blue Aston Martin Vanquish. The car only had delivery mileage on the clock, and he'd only driven the car twice since the day he had taken delivery of it; he thought of it more as an investment.

George came from a working-class family where there was lots of love but little money. His father couldn't drive, and his mother had briefly owned a Ford Popular car that had been bought on finance, which they really couldn't afford. Even this had been repossessed after they'd defaulted on the payment. He told himself that he'd bought the Aston Martin as an investment but the real reason he had bought it was because he could!

He carefully replaced the cover over the Aston Martin. He took the blue plastic bag containing the bread, milk and eggs he'd bought at the service station from the passenger footwell of the Mondeo'. He grabbed his suitcase and his blue RAF bag from the boot and made his way to a key coded door in the garage that led into the main house.

He went into the kitchen, put the food away and carried his luggage upstairs to the master bedroom, placing the bags at the end of the bed. He got undressed, took a shower and changed into his sleep shorts then flopped onto his king-size bed. The thoughts going round in his head were constant and as he tried to relax and close his eyes, the main thought which entered his head was—: how had he become involved in smuggling drugs?

He hadn't joined the RAF to do this and there was no justifying his involvement. Occasionally, he would try to ease his conscience by donating money to local charities, but this didn't help. He was now a major drug importer and to make matters worse, it had been all his idea. He tried to dismiss his train of thought completely but he couldn't; he was in too deep. Finally, the tiredness from the journey home and the strain of what he'd done hit him. He'd been running on adrenaline since the ferry had docked at Felixstowe and he was exhausted. As he lay on the bed, he let the blackness envelop him and he fell into a deep sleep.

The next morning after waking early, which he was conditioned to do, he went back to the garage and carefully removed the back seat from the Mondeo by removing six screws from a small, welded plate that was carefully hidden under the seat. He removed the foam packing and took out ten double vacuumed sealed plastic bags of cocaine each weighing 1 kilo. He placed the bags into a haversack and carefully replaced the foam packaging and the car seat. He took the drugs back into the house and went back to his bedroom where he concealed them in a purpose-built compartment located in the floor of his walk-in wardrobe. Before he took a shower, he looked at himself in the mirror and he didn't like what he saw looking back at him! He saw a middle-aged man of roughly six feet in height with brown hair and eyes and a slightly out-of-condition body. *Nothing special* he thought to himself. He used to be so into his sport and keeping fit. He made a mental note to do more exercise and not to look in a full-length mirror for a while.

He showered and had some breakfast of scrambled eggs on toast and a coffee. He got dressed and started to give some thought to how and where he would meet his middleman, a man whom George called 'the chameleon'.

It had been three months since George's last home leave and as well as meeting the man who moved the cocaine on for them, he also had his real friends and family to call in on. For the last sixteen months, Flight Sergeant George Stewart had organised and been involved with a small but very efficient military drug-smuggling ring. All four men involved had made vast amounts of money, which was wrong but was a highly successful operation that was run with military precision and detailed planning. The sad fact was all four men involved were at the top of their game. If they had put as much effort into running a legitimate business outside of their military smuggling operation, it would have been one of the top one hundred blue-chip companies in the UK within the same short time scale.

George Stewart and his military smuggling partners rarely took the risks that he'd undertaken on this trip home. He had a middleman who disposed of the cocaine for them and had an immediate cash buyer for all the ten kilos. Their contact had done business with this man before and had assured George he'd a good business track record and always paid on delivery. They also had the promise of more orders, and it wasn't easy finding men with the resources and the amounts of ready cash at their disposal to buy large quantities of cocaine in the UK.

George had never been stopped or even searched by customs on his many previous home-leave visits. He'd moved large quantities of cocaine through their middleman, receiving payment directly into bank accounts and then moving the money quickly to other hard-to-trace accounts once the transactions were complete. George had never got involved with selling the product personally, as he wasn't *that* stupid. He dropped it at different pre-arranged spots that he'd picked out himself and the middleman collected it and did the rest.

The middleman was unaware of George's personal details and was also aware that he was paid extremely well for finding a buyer, making the delivery and not asking any awkward questions.

The normal way of getting the cocaine into the country was to fly or ship the consignment in amongst military cargo. All four men were strategically placed to do this and had agreed to a two-year plan at the very start. They'd decided to import as much cocaine as was possible without taking unnecessary risks and then take early retirement. They would buy themselves out of their remaining military service and live the rest of their lives in luxury. They had all been volunteers when joining the military, which meant it was possible to buy the remaining years of their service. It would mean reduced pensions but that would be the least of their worries if everything went according to plan.

They were now sixteen months into the plan and everything was running exactly as was planned. It was funny how the smallest of details can start to unravel the most intricate plans. Being military men, they all had a fall-back position and George was very soon about to find out just how necessary this fall-back position was.

Chapter 3
The Supply Route

On a week's holiday in the coastal region of Galicia in Spain, George met a man who was ultimately destined to change his life and the lives of his three friends and colleagues in a way that was beyond anything that they could have imagined. He had travelled to the Spanish resort of Sanxenxo with his good friend, Petty Officer Paul Wilson, for a week of rest and relaxation. During the one-hour transfer from Santiago de Compostela Airport to their hotel in Sanxenxo they had talked about the following day's fishing trip that George had organised for them. They had discussed who was going to catch the biggest fish.

"It's great to spend a week with you Paul, you old pirate."

"Never mind all that, George, just tell me how you plan to spoil me for the week?"

George just smiled and said, "I'll start by making you late for everything, as I know how you love being late."

Paul frowned as his condition of allegro phobia was brought up, but then he laughed as he said, "Just don't be late getting to the bar while we're on this holiday."

Paul Wilson had suffered the longest travelling time of the journey to their holiday destination. He had travelled from Plymouth to Frankfurt, met George at Frankfurt Airport and then they'd caught a flight to Spain. Paul was really tired after travelling for the best part of the day. George was already based in Germany, so he had only travelled about half a day to meet up and travel with his good friend to Spain. Both men enjoyed each other's company, and they were in good spirits looking forward to their week's holiday. They decided on a thirty-euro wager for who caught the biggest fish the following day.

The following morning, both men woke at their usual time of six a.m. in their hotel. This was despite them staying up drinking in the hotel bar until one a.m. After showering and dressing their adjacent hotel rooms, they went down to the hotel reception together. It was too early for breakfast and the dining room wasn't open until seven-thirty a.m. which was just as well as they were both nursing major hangovers. They made their way out to the front of the hotel for the seven a.m. pick up. The man who picked them up in his Suzuki Jeep was a tanned and lean Spaniard with a slightly weathered face; he spoke surprisingly good English. "Hi, I'm Jorgé', you must be George." He extended his hand to Paul Wilson who was sitting on the bench.

"I'm Paul, he's George," he said, pointing to George sitting with his eyes closed and his cap pulled down over his eyes. "And you're late Jorgé."

"He's just a grumpy old git! I'm George, and we're ready to catch some big ones! Lead the way."

Jorgé invited both men to climb into the Jeep, which they did and he drove off. George was in the passenger seat as they drove the few miles from their hotel to the wharf in the Port of Meloxo, where their fishing boat was moored and kitted out ready for their fishing trip. On arrival at the wharf, George was impressed with his first sight of the fishing boat: it was a thirty-foot twin-hulled boat with two powerful outboard engines on the rear and the whole rig looked fairly new. *Not your usual old fishing boat,* George thought to himself. The sign painted on the side said *"The Blumare Nautico."*

As the men climbed aboard, a slightly nauseous George said, "I'm impressed with your boat, Jorgé."

"You can be impressed later if we catch anything," was Jorgé's smiling response.

It was Paul's turn to speak now he looked at the colour draining from George's face and said, "I hope you've got lots of water for our flyboy here Jorgé; he's not used to sailing or fishing."

George said, "I feel sick already!"

'Jorgé looked at George and said, "I've brought lots of beer, wine and water as well as food for our lunch. Looking at you, George, we might just need the water on this trip."

Both Paul and Jorgé were smiling as the fishing boat pulled out of the harbour and George started groaning. "What was our bet again George!" was the last thing Paul said as Jorgé opened up the two engines and the fishing boat sped out towards the Island of Arousa. After fishing for a few hours anchored four miles off the coast, Paul had caught a couple of small bream, and a decent-sized *maragota* which Jorgé had told them was called a wrasse in English. George had caught nothing and had been sick on two occasions. Fishing and being on the water definitely weren't George's thing.

They pulled anchor and sailed to the pretty little Island of Arouse where they again dropped anchor at a small cove with a white sandy beach. Jorgé prepared lunch while George and Paul went for a swim in the beautiful crystal-clear waters surrounding the island.

Swimming and having some lunch made George feel better.

For the final two hours of their fishing trip, George was getting a little bit bored, and he still hadn't caught a fish. He finally admitted defeat and stopped fishing. He reeled in and put his fishing rod down on the deck. This left the angling to Paul and George, who was now ready to go back, said, "I'll pay the thirty euros gladly if we can go home now."

Paul, who was enjoying himself fishing, said, "Give me one more hour and we'll head back in."

George resignedly said "Okay," and went and sat in the boat wheelhouse with Jorgé.

The two men seemed relaxed in each other's company. "Where did you learn to speak English Jorgé? You speak English really well, but I can't quite place your accent though."

'Jorgé smiled at George and said, "Thanks. My father is from Galicia and my mum is a Geordie! She moved here from Newcastle after meeting my dad twenty-five years ago. She still says she's waiting to see if it works out!" Both men laughed loudly at this.

The light was fading as the fishing boat pulled into the harbour and Paul was fast asleep on the bench. George looked at him and said "The travelling to get here and the late drinking session last night has wiped him out. "Looks like I'll be stuck in our hotel bar on my own tonight."

'Jorgé said, "I'll show you around a few bars if your friend is too tired to go out." He gave George a business card containing an advert for his fishing business and his mobile phone number. As Jorgé dropped them back off at their hotel he said, "If you want to meet later for a drink, give me a ring."

They both climbed out of the Jeep and Jorgé drove off. George said to Paul, "Let's go to the bar and spend your thirty-euro winnings mate before you fall asleep on me again!"

After a few drinks in the hotel bar, they made their way to the lift and on their way up to the room, Paul was already yawning.

George said, "Look mate, you're wiped out from all the travelling, you have an early night, and we can pick up the holiday fun again tomorrow morning."

Paul, who was feeling drained, said, "If you're good with that, I'm out on my feet mate."

George pre-empted Paul's next question by saying, "Don't worry about it, I'll take our friend Jorgé up on his offer to show me around."

Chapter 4
The Proposition

George rang Jorgé's mobile phone number and he answered straight away. They arranged to meet at the hotel bar at seven-thirty p.m. He had time to have a quick shower, change his clothes and get a light meal from the hotel dining room. *I don't need to be drinking on an empty stomach tonight or there will be two of us wasted on this holiday by tomorrow morning,* George thought to himself.

He was already sitting at the bar having his first drink when Jorgé turned up. George asked him what he wanted to drink and he said, "I'll have what you are drinking."

George ordered him a large brandy and said, "We'd better introduce ourselves properly, Jorgé. I know you know my name is George Stewart and whose company have I got the pleasure of tonight?"

"I'm Jorgé Calmez and I'm half-Spanish and half-Geordie and unlike you George, I'm all 'fisherman'." They both laughed.

After finishing their drinks, Jorgé took George to a local bar, "La Bombilla", which in English means, 'The Light Bulb'. While there, George was introduced to a couple of Jorgé's friends, A'lvaro and Rodrigo. They seemed like nice lads and the four men started to have a laugh about George's non-existent sea legs and his seasickness on the boat trip. The atmosphere was nice and relaxed and although Jorgé's friends didn't speak English nearly as well as Jorgé, George managed to make himself understood with only the occasional translation from Jorgé. They treated him more like a friend of Jorgé's instead of a tourist and he started to relax and really enjoy the evening.

After they had their fourth round of drinks, Jorgé asked George if he could have a quiet word. They took their drinks to a corner table in the bar to talk but George was wondering what Jorgé wanted to discuss privately.

'Jorgé spoke in a quiet voice. "What is it that you and Paul do for a living?"

George said, "We are both in the military, why do you ask?"

'Jorgé could see that George was getting a little uneasy with the conversation, so he chose his next words carefully. "I just wanted to give you a proposition!"

"What kind of proposition?" George replied.

"The kind where we could both make a lot of money."

"Does this involve me giving you money, Jorgé?"

"No, it doesn't; I'm not trying to rip you off, George. I'm really serious; we could both make a lot of money very quickly."

George Stewart was certainly no fool and he certainly wasn't a man to get stung, but the conversation was interesting him now.

"You don't look like you're short of a few quid Jorgé". "Your boat is nearly new. But anyway, how could we make this money?"

'Jorgé replied succinctly, "Cocaine."

There was a silence.

"Just hear me out before you say anything. I can get the cocaine into Galicia, but I need a business partner who can distribute it for me, someone I could trust, George, someone like you and your friend Paul."

George was shocked at being offered this proposition but found himself saying, "You don't know anything about me! You could be talking to a policeman right now."

'Jorgé looked at him and simply said, "I'm not though, am I? I need to take a chance on someone who could organise a regular distribution route and become a trusted partner; a man who is smart and has the skills to make this happen without getting us caught. A man like you, George. At the moment, it's just me and a friend; we have already got the first shipment ready to go, but we need a person like you to distribute and sell it. If you agreed to join us you would not need to put any money in; we would do a trial run first once you had a chance to organise things. If your friend Paul wants to be a partner, then this would be okay with us. Are you both in the army?" "No Jorgé we're not, I'm in the air force and Paul is in the navy. I need a moment to take all this in."

Although George found himself interested in what Jorgé was saying, he was no longer relaxed and was now very wary and in a state of alertness. The thought of making enough money to get out of the RAF to do what he wanted while there was still time to enjoy life kept him interested. "This might sound like a stupid question Jorgé, but where does the cocaine come from?"

'Jorgé replied, "So you are at least interested?"

George just smiled and said, "We're only talking, Jorgé."

"It comes from Colombia, and it's taken overland from there to the Port of New Amsterdam in Guyana; and from there it's loaded onto a ship, which makes the three-thousand-five-hundred-mile voyage and then drops anchor offshore. And finally, it's transferred to me on the *Blumare* about twenty miles out. I bring it into Pontevedra and land it in one of the many quiet estuaries. I know this coastline like the back of my hand. I'm telling you all of this to show you I trust you, George, and I'm taking a big leap of faith in you."

George couldn't really believe what he was being asked in this little Spanish bar, but it did all sound feasible. "I don't know what to say, Jorgé."

'Jorgé said, "Don't say anything; talk it over with Paul. If you're interested, ring me tomorrow and I will take you to my house and show you the cocaine I have, for the first trial run." George found himself saying, "I'll speak to Paul, but even if I can convince him to be part of what you are suggesting, it will take time for us to set things up. I would need to plan things properly and it would take time for us to find the right buyers. There are lots of risks to all of this, Jorgé."

'Jorgé nodded as he replied, "There are some risks as you say, but you seem like a man who could minimise those risks, that's why I chose you."

George said, "Yes Jorgé that and the fact that you've found no one else stupid enough!"

Both men laughed.

"But remember, George, if we get this right there are also massive rewards for all of us."

George shrugged his shoulders and said, "I'm promising you nothing Jorgé."

"Okay, George, if I don't get a call off you tomorrow, then I'll know you are not interested in quickly becoming a millionaire."

Neither could help quietly laughing at Jorgé's last comment.

As the evening ended and George walked back to the hotel, he wondered how to broach the subject of him and his best friend Paul both respectable military men now becoming drug smugglers. *He will probably tell me "to go fuck myself" and he would be right. The money would allow us to live a little and I could buy myself out of the RAF and retire in luxury if I could make this work,* he thought to himself. He liked Jorgé and his friends he'd met that night, and it was true that Jorgé had taken a chance on George being the man to get involved with him in this mad scheme. The thought of becoming a drug smuggler even for a short time was a big moral dilemma to him, but the pull of making millions of pounds and realising his dreams was just too strong and could become a very real possibility. It suddenly occurred to him just how he might convince Paul to be involved. If it worked out, Paul would be able to buy his own sailing boat. He was always harping on about owning his dream sailing yacht.

The following morning at breakfast, Paul was full of beans; he was refreshed after his early night and ready to go. "How did your night go with Jorgé and the locals? George just ignored the question. "What shall we do today, Georgie Boy? I fancy going to the beach and looking at the nice *senoritas!*"

George was just drinking his coffee; he knew there wasn't going to be a good time to tell Paul what Jorgé had asked them to become involved in. "Last night was interesting, to say the least. We ended up at a local bar and met a couple of Jorgé's friends. I've got something I want to ask you mate!"

Paul listened to what George was telling him, without

saying a word and at the end of it, he said "Are you out of your mind George! We're not drug smugglers! And even if we wanted to be, we don't know anyone to sell a large amount of cocaine to."

George looked at his friend in the eyes and said, "Well that's not strictly true, I know a friend back in Liverpool whom I trust and who will find us a buyer. All I'm saying, Paul, is that I've been in the RAF for sixteen years and I still haven't got a pot to piss in."

Paul said, "But you've got your house."

"I've got a large mortgage on the house." was George's response. "I don't want to retire in a few years and be scratching around. You are in the same boat as me, mate. You are not exactly rolling in money yourself." It was then that he played his ace. "If we made this work out, even for a short time, you could buy that sailing boat that you've always wanted. All I'm asking is that we meet him and see what he's got to say."

There was a long pause before Paul broke his silence, "I trust you, George, and if you think we have a chance of making a lot of money, then there's no harm in listening to what Jorgé has got to say. If for one second, I think he's dodgy or full of shit George, we are out."

George couldn't believe he had managed to get Paul on board. "I'll make the call." That's how it all started.

George made the call and Jorgé was pleased he had phoned. "I take it Paul is interested then, George?" He's interested in making lots of money quickly as long as we don't get caught."

"Same as me George, it's something we all agree on, I will come and pick you both up at the hotel in one hour."

"Jorgé when you take us to your house to discuss things, make sure your partner is there too. I'd like to get to know everyone and everything from the start, especially those who we might do business with." "Okay, George but you have already met my partner, Rodrigo. He agreed to let me bring you both to La Bombilla. I told him we could trust you and Paul. And like your friend trusts you, Rodrigo trusts my judgement. You are not the only one who needs their friend's approval, George."

One hour later Jorgé and Rodrigo turned up in the Suzuki Jeep and picked them both up from the hotel. George recognised Rodrigo and introduced him to Paul. Jorgé took them on a twenty-minute drive from the hotel in Sanxenxo to the Poio area and the little coastal town of Combarro. When they reached Combarro, they drove for a couple of minutes down a few narrow quiet little lanes and stopped at a rustic traditional stone cottage situated on the edge of the town. It was a quiet and secluded place and wasn't overlooked by other properties.

"This is my home George, that I've brought you and Paul to. My girlfriend is staying with her mother for a couple of days, so we won't be disturbed at all. We all have to start by trusting each other in a short space of time, for this to work. This is why I have brought you to my home to show you both that Rodrigo and I trust in you both already."

The four men got out and entered the cottage which was tastefully furnished with local traditional Galician furniture, and it had a woman's touch about the place. Jorgé invited George and Paul to take a seat and make themselves comfortable and asked Rodrigo to pour them all a drink from bottles of white wine in the cabinet in the front room. Rodrigo came back a few minutes later with a small canvas holdall containing eight one-kilo packages of the finest pure Colombian cocaine wrapped tightly in heavy-duty polythene bags and secured with tape.

"This is what we will trust you with on the trial run, gentlemen," he said, and he handed a tightly wrapped kilo bag each to George and Paul. This now made the proposition very real to both men.

George and Paul now knew that Jorgé and Rodrigo's were serious. George wanted to know what they would make from becoming involved in the smuggling of cocaine. His first question to Jorgé was, "How much have you paid to get the eight kilos to Galicia?"

Jorgé addressed his comments to both George and Paul, "It costs us twenty-eight thousand dollars which is about twenty-two thousand pounds. It would cost us double this if we hadn't brought some in on the *Blumare* for someone else. It costs seven thousand dollars a kilo to buy it directly from the Port in Guyana and get it shipped across the Atlantic for collection by us. But that kilo you have in your hand, George, is eighty-five per cent pure. By the time it is sold on the streets in the UK it will be cut to just thirty per cent. If you can get it into the UK, they will line up to buy that kilo off you for a minimum of seventy thousand pounds." Jorgé addressed both George and Paul when he said, "It adds up to us all becoming very rich men in a very short space of time."

Paul spoke next. "Only if we can find a way to get it in the UK, and only if we can find a regular buyer for it without getting caught."

George chimed in with, "If we did this, it would take very careful planning and we would need time to find the right people to sell it to."

Jorgé looked at Rodrigo and said, "I told you these were the right men. George — Paul, take as much time as you like to organise your end of the agreement. Let's see if this trial run works first. And when it does work, which I know it will, we will want our twenty thousand pounds back and we can then split the rest four ways. We are putting a lot of trust in each other." Jorgé looked around at all of them.

George then spoke, "How would you feel about splitting the money six ways instead of four?"

Jorgé asked, "Why six ways?"

George answered, "To make this work, I'd need to recruit two other men. We want to start off by being honest with each other, right?" Both Jorgé and Rodrigo nodded. "Well, I will need another two men who I work with to come on board to make this all happened. Without these other two men, Paul and I couldn't do it without taking too big a risk. No matter what the rewards are, a six-way split is still a massive amount of money each if we set a pipeline up. And to be honest, if I can't get these other two men to come on board, it's not going work anyway!"

Jorgé looked at Rodrigo and he nodded approval. "Looks like there will be six men involved. Go and recruit the rest of the team, and then let us know when you are ready for the trial run."

Jorgé proposed a toast "To us and our new enterprise gentlemen."

All four men raised their glasses and said in unison, "To us!"

Chapter 5
The Team

In every successful business, be it legitimate or criminal, there is always a driving force, a man or woman who guides the business to success or failure. In The 'Organisation' this man was Flight Sergeant George Stewart. It was he who came up with the idea of the military smuggling ring. It was also he who had worked out a way of getting the cocaine into the country undetected by air and sea and it was also George Stewart who would eventually find the required buyers for the smuggled cocaine in the UK

George Stewart was a highly intelligent man but a very flawed individual. He had come from a working-class background which had instilled in him a need to acquire life's unnecessary things, things like a big house or an expensive car. He wrongly based the acquisition of these things as the measure of a man's success in life, he had already forged a successful military career, but this was not enough for him he wanted the finer things in life, luxuries which the money he was now earning from the smuggling ring would allow him to buy.

He could plan complex travel and logistical movements coupled with his meticulous eye for detail; this is what had enabled him to gain promotions and rise through the non-commissioned ranks in the RAF With his drive and attention to detail, he was a man who was able to run a very successful business in civilian life if chose too. George was a realist and knew that he wasn't able to do everything on his own. In any successful enterprise, a specialised team was needed, and he knew exactly who the specialised team was going to be, in this particular criminal enterprise. His reasoning was to try to keep the numbers to a minimum as it would be much less complicated and there would be less of a chance of something going wrong. He already had his friend Paul Wilson involved but he needed another two military men for it all to work. It was the lure of the millions of pounds that tempted the other two men to join them.

The smuggling ring that all four men called 'The Organisation' was now made up of a team of experienced military men who were all experts in their chosen fields that involved them moving military equipment and logistics worldwide and this could happen at a moment's notice. The team consisted of three serving RAF men and one senior non-commissioned officer serving in the Royal Navy. Three of the men were senior non-commissioned officers and one held the Queen's commission at the rank of Squadron Leader. None of the men was the type who you would expect to be involved in smuggling drugs, and for this very reason, they were all allowed to carry out various roles in the organisation without coming under any suspicion by their colleagues.

It wasn't easy to convince the other three military members to become part of the team, but George Stewart was close to his commanding officer. They had become good friends and he was already aware that Squadron Leader Walker was a man who was floundering in a sea of debt thanks to his wife's 'devil-may-care' attitude to spending money. His wife was a very beautiful woman who regularly threatened to leave him. She was ruthless when it came to spending money. She was always pushing him to buy a big, detached house and to get them both luxury cars and expensive jewellery for her. He simply could not afford the lifestyle she demanded he provides on his RAF salary but he was desperate for her to stay with him.

When George Stewart tentatively approached David Walker with his drug-smuggling scheme which would allow him to rapidly get very rich it was at a time when David would have sold his soul to the devil as a way to absolve himself of the debt and at the same time satisfy his demanding wife. He had managed to keep his debts secret from his superiors, but he found the constant worry kept him awake at night. David took little convincing when his flight sergeant asked him to have a private conversation, he told his other non-commissioned officers he wasn't to be disturbed as the two men sat down in his office.

"What did you want to speak to me about that had to be so private, George?"

"It's about changing both our lives, David." Both men were used to being on first-name terms when they were on their own.

"Changing both our lives, George? Don't tell me you have won the football pools and you are giving me half of your winnings! Whatever you are about to say won't be enough to change my life at the moment I'm afraid. As you know I'm in serious debt."

"Winning the football pools is not what I wanted to tell you David, but it does involve us both getting a lot of money quickly."

David Walker's interest was a little keener now. "Go on then, George, I'm all ears."

"What I'm about to tell you, David, you are not going to like."

David replied, "I don't like the fact that I am already involved by the sound of it."

George continued "If you do decide to be a part of what I am about to tell you, we will both be millionaires within the next two years. You can settle all of your debt and live very well indeed until the end of your RAF career."

David's response was "So I can leave the RAF a millionaire and live the rest of my life in luxury! Who do we have to kill, George." he said only half-jokingly. David was about to say something else, but George held up his hand to stop him from speaking.

"Let me finish telling you what I have to say, David, then I will listen to you afterwards I promise." George went on to tell him about the cocaine supply route from Colombia to Guyana and then on to Galicia in Spain. He told him how he proposed to get it into the UK by air and occasionally by sea and by using his navy friend, Paul Wilson and Sergeant Mark Watton based at Cosford, he explained how he needed to recruit somebody to sell it on their behalf at a vast profit. He held nothing back in his explanation, giving his detailed plan of how he intended to smuggle the drugs while pointing out the consequences of them being caught and even telling him that he already had eight kilos, ready to be smuggled into the UK and sold on. George knew that without David's help to sign his transport and movement orders in and out of RAF Brüggen, the whole operation would be a non-starter. He spoke at length without interruption from David Walker for about thirty minutes before he finally stopped talking and said, "That it! That's the plan, David. It's not something I would have ever thought about getting involved in or asking you to do the same, but it is the only way I know how to guarantee both of us leaving the RAF with enough money to live our lives in total luxury."

David Walker was shocked by what George had told him but when he next spoke it was going to be George's turn to be a little shocked by his reply. "You wouldn't be expecting me to give you this answer, but you can count me in! As bad as your drug-smuggling ring sounds, it's the only lifeline I've got of staying in the RAF and keeping my commission. I am in hundreds of thousands of pounds worth of debt. We both know why I'm in debt, but I love her. It's only a matter of time before my debts are discovered and I'm asked to resign my commission because of the mess I'm in. That's all I need to say about my predicament, George. If this organisation of yours has any chance of working, it would be my only way out of this mess, so I'm definitely in. We need to go through your plans again very carefully."

George just smiled and said, "It's going to work, David and we will only have to do it for a short period to get very rich."

As David Walker had said, he was in a mountain of debt thanks to his greedy wife. He was a short, plain looking and boring type of man who had gone as far as he was going to go up the RAF chain of command. The woman he was married to was very beautiful, but she was a woman who had developed a taste for the high life and very expensive things, and this had all worked to George's advantage when asking David to become involved in the smuggling ring. He couldn't have timed it better when he asked David to become involved as, in David Walker's eyes, he had no other way out of debt and to make matters even worse he'd fathered two daughters who were now both at an age where he now needed to help them financially through university. For numerous wrong reasons, Squadron Leader David Walker was now a member and George knew he had recruited one of the most important needed members of the team.

The four men had many years' service between them: two of them, Flight Sergeant George Stewart and Sergeant Mark Watton, had joined the RAF at the same time and were both on the same basic training course at RAF Swinderby in Lincolnshire. George Stewart was based at RAF Brüggen in the transport and logistics section where Squadron Leader David Walker was his commanding officer and effectively his boss. Sergeant Mark Watton had met and liked the other three men, and he also worked in transport and logistics and was based at RAF Cosford situated near Walsall and Birmingham in the West Midlands. RAF Cosford was a relatively small and quiet RAF training base used to train engineering staff and administration personnel. It still had logistical flights flying in and out of RAF Cosford which moved equipment to both military bases at home and abroad daily. In addition, it had excellent sports training facilities and a large indoor sports arena located in an annexed part of the base where occasionally they would hold national athletic meetings which were open to the public.

Cosford also housed the RAF Museum in a separate area attached to the airbase and where public access was allowed. Although security on the base itself was high and access to the base was not allowed by uninvited delivery staff or civilian personnel, the attached museum and sports arena areas were both easily accessible to the serving RAF personnel on the base and usually without any checks at all for senior non-commissioned officers. This made it an ideal base for the organisation's purpose; if something was flown into the country on a military transport aircraft and then needed to be picked up and transported by road from the base, this was easily arranged.

Chief Petty Officer Paul Wilson of the Royal Navy was based at HMNB Devonport in Plymouth and was the only member of the team who was not in the RAF He worked in transport and logistics and had been seconded to Customs and Excise on several occasions making him a very valued member of the team. He'd met George Stewart when they were both signed up for the same three-week joint services parachute course being held at Lippspringe army base in Germany. This was a British Army base where they both got ribbed by the army lads on the course and because of this, both men stuck together. After the course had ended, they kept in touch and had done so for the last ten years resulting in them becoming close friends, as well as now being smuggling partners.

All four men had exemplary military records and had seen action whilst on active service around the world. They were in conflicts in Iraq, Iran and Afghanistan and other areas in the Middle East. This made their involvement and being members of this particular team even more strange. It was too late to pull out for all of them now. They had all been brave and loyal and served their country well, but for the last sixteen months they had all turned into criminal drug smugglers and each one of them was doing it for the money.

Each man had decided to become involved with the organisation at a reflective time in their lives, all trying to make sense of what, if anything, they had achieved. It was hard for men who had chosen careers to serve their country to come to terms with what they were actually doing. They all still did their respective jobs and got good ratings in their periodic six-monthly reports which all servicemen have to be assessed by. In fact, it made sense to continue to do their jobs well and not to arouse suspicion as all four men were now putting a lot more of their energy and time into their own personal enterprise.

All of them wanted to quickly earn a great amount of money and the two-year time limit they had all agreed on seemed overly long to George, but he also knew that it wasn't an enterprise to rush. They couldn't make any mistakes; the rewards were unbelievable but so were the consequences of any of them getting caught.

Each man had wrestled with his conscience regarding what they had to do to achieve their goals over the two years and from the very beginning, it was agreed by all four men that 10% of any money made would be donated to their respective military charities. In Paul Wilson's case that meant 10% of his money being donated to the Royal Navy Benevolent Fund and each of the other three would each donate 10% each to the RAF Benevolent Fund. It was a meaningless gesture considering how they were earning the money to make the donations but strangely, it made all the men feel better about what they were doing.

Not one of the four men earned enough money to fund their lifestyles: Squadron Leader David Walker had two girls going through university in Edinburgh where his home was, he also had a villa in the Algarve in Portugal along with his now substantial bank account. His villa in Portugal was to be his bolthole should anything go wrong. Petty Officer Paul Wilson was in the midst of a messy and expensive divorce which was a kind of an occupational hazard in the forces; he still liked to live well, and he was living for the day he could leave the navy and buy his own sailing boat.

Sergeant Mark Watton's problem was that he liked to gamble, badly as it turned out. He really needed help for his habit which of course he was never going to receive; the horses were his particular poison, but he would gamble on any sporting event.

Flight Sergeant George Stewart liked the most expensive things that money could buy, like his Aston Martin, although he had never really driven it for any length of time, he just enjoyed the feeling of owning it. He was also fond of good food and wine and expensive clothes, but not jewellery. No, that would draw attention and he was careful enough never to show his expensive tastes whilst at his place of work. He appeared to his air-force colleagues to live quite moderately and this was something he always asked the other three men to adhere to.

George tried hard to keep his military and civilian life apart with a great deal of success. He had signed on for twelve years in the RAF and when he had served his twelve years, he had re-signed for a further six years taking him to eighteen years in total. He now only had six months left of this term to reach the eighteen years that he had signed on for. George still wanted to leave the RAF now more than ever despite him being offered a promotion to become a warrant officer. He didn't want to sign on for another four years to take him to the maximum full twenty-two years military term. George loved the life in the services but believed that the RAF was starting to do his thinking for him, and he wanted to experience new things in life. Even before the drug-smuggling operation had begun, he had decided to leave at the end of his eighteen years and retire on a reduced pension. He now had the money and the opportunity to do what he wanted.

The four men all had things in common, one of the biggest things that had influenced them all to get involved with the smuggling operation was that they had all seen comrades injured in action, and they had seen how their wounded friends and comrades were treated by the military. Some of these people had mental conditions and were thrown out of the services with little counselling or training and then forgotten about and thrown on the scrap heap of life. Some of these men were just left to fend for themselves in civilian life and each and every one of them was suffering from post-traumatic stress disorder. This usually gave them no chance of leading productive lives and earning a decent living outside the military; they were just abandoned.

Of course, this alone did not justify what they were doing; all four were intelligent men and all four of them knew that all this changed very little as they all remained drug dealers and there was nothing that could change that fact. At least when they left the services, they would all leave rich men and they all figured they had earned a well-provisioned early retirement.

It eased their consciences a little to think that part of their ill-gotten gains was being donated back to help some of their comrades and they allowed themselves to believe, rightly or wrongly, that the end justified the means. It didn't, of course, it just made them all feel a little bit better and let's be honest the money was good, extremely good. The four men tried to meet up once every two months, leave permitting, but all four men kept in communication frequently or when required using burner phones. A burner phone was a cheap mobile phone used only once or twice at the most and then disposed of, they were all aware of the ability to track and monitor conversations. David Walker and George Stewart had worked at a secret underground military listening base just outside Maastricht in Holland and both men were aware of surveillance techniques and the need for utmost secrecy in their endeavours.

The proceeds of any drug runs were split into six separate parts: two shares were given to Jorgé and Rodrigo in Spain and 10% of the remainder was deducted and paid anonymously to the four men's respected military charities after which the remaining money was split into four equal parts and then paid into the men's own numbered Swiss bank accounts. They kept a running float of around one million pounds in a separate offshore account and that money was available for purchasing the cocaine and oiling the transportation wheels where necessary. This particular offshore account was sent up in the name of a bogus Ltd company that George had purchased legally but in a false name. It was an off-the-shelf limited company that came ready to trade complete with fake directors. From this account, all four men could access the money it contained when required, which enabled them to run the operation smoothly and efficiently.

Chapter 6
Controlled Entry

It was already the job of the four men to move men as well as military equipment in and out of the country rapidly with very short notice. Three of the men were in high positions within the RAF supply and logistics chain and Paul Wilson was a senior NCO in the Royal Navy which was the perfect cover to run a drug-smuggling operation.

Men follow orders to the letter in the British military and no one ever questions superior officer's orders or dares to even ask why. Flight Sergeant George Stewart and Squadron Leader David Walker at RAF Brüggen could carry out their part of the smuggling operation with relative impunity.

As the commissioned officer in charge of supplies, David Walker issued the orders and his senior NCO, George Stewart, made sure that they were carried out to the letter ensuring no outside interference from other officers. They always made sure that their regular RAF supply and logistical duties were carried out efficiently and the regular monthly audits were all kept up to date with their section stock and man movement all nicely accounted for. This ensured no interference and that they could continue their own operation undisturbed. They were highly commended by the station commander for the way their section was being run.

The two men were ideally placed to be successful drug

smugglers and to get rich quickly whilst maintaining the pipeline for the cocaine to enter the UK while also ensuring they stayed undetected. They virtually had carte blanche to do as they wished provided that they paid attention to the details and ensured that the section's mundane tasks were completed daily. They joked with each other that the only thing that could really shut them down immediately was if the Russians attacked!

On this particular morning, David Walker had sent an airman to find George and ask him to attend a meeting in his office. He found George checking the inventory of a recent air freight consignment. On arrival at the office, David was sitting at his desk studying a piece of paper and he looked worried. "Come in George and close the door behind you. We've got a bit of a problem!"

George replied, "What kind of a problem?"

David handed George a piece of paper he was holding. "This kind of problem." "It is an official request from the station commander for me to find and appoint a warrant officer to our supply and logistics section on the base. I have to appoint a senior non-commissioned officer to our section. It's something I have been meaning to do and I should have done it months ago."

George took a moment to digest what this meant and replied, "Yes I can see why this would be a problem for us. "If we have a warrant officer on this section, he will have to know all of our transport movements."

David Walker spoke in a lower tone now. "My hands are tied, and I don't have a choice but to appoint someone. There is, however, a solution that could solve our problem." George frowned and listened to David's solution. "I will recommend *you* for promotion to warrant officer, George. I'm sure the station commander will approve it and it would stop anyone else coming in and interfering with our plans."

George was deep in thought.

"Well, what do you think?" David asked him.

"I think it would be an ideal solution if I was staying in the RAF, but I'm not planning to. You know my plan is to buy myself out on medical grounds for my last remaining years of service."

David looked perplexed and said, "Medical grounds? You are fit as a fiddle. How are you going to swing that?"

George smiled and said, "Diabetes and blood pressure; I've already got the doctor on my side. He thinks I've only got months to live!"

Both men started laughing.

George continued "If everything goes to plan, I will only be coming out with a couple of months service left to do. That's the reason why I'm doing this. How would it look if you promote me and then I apply to leave the RAF?"

David just shrugged and said, "It wouldn't look good I suppose. Men close to retirement would give their right arm for a promotion like this, you know that, George."

George replied, "Yes I know David and I would get a higher pension too with that promotion, but you and I are not going to need to rely on the RAF pension are we!"

David stood up and looked out of his office window "Well what is the solution then, George? One way or another he wants a warrant officer appointed here to our section." George said, "Look, David, tell the station commander that you are already considering me for the promotion, but you are still assessing me; at least that way it will keep him off your back for a few months. If it gets to the point of him insisting on you having a warrant officer for the section immediately, I suppose I will just have to accept the promotion and we can get a new Flight Sergeant. That way we can stick the new recruit in a separate office and keep his nose out of our business."

Both men laughed out loud this time. They didn't know whether they were laughing at the absurdity of George not wanting to be promoted or at their general situation.

Squadron Leader David Walker had declined several attempts to have a warrant officer assigned to his section for obvious reasons, he argued successfully to his station commander that his Flight Sergeant George Stewart was exceptional, and he was recommending him for a promotion to warrant officer very shortly and it was hard to argue against this line of reasoning as the supply and logistics section at RAF Brüggen was indeed run very efficiently.

This meant that as the senior non-commissioned transport and logistics officer at RAF Brüggen, one of the main jobs of Flight Sergeant George Stewart was to make cargo and customs checks on all incoming and outgoing logistical flights entering or leaving the base.

George had worked out from the planning stage that for the men to run a highly successful drug-smuggling operation and more importantly to not be detected while doing so that a sophisticated way of smuggling the drugs into the UK would have to be found. The method of getting the cocaine onto the aircraft and off again to be loaded on a separate flight back to the UK would need to be foolproof and uncomplicated. All incoming aircraft to the base from another country received standard spot checks sometimes by the RAF military police or

RAF regiment airmen using dogs and if anything was found during one of these checks, it would jeopardise the whole operation. He needed to devise a simple and direct way to effectively load and then send the cocaine from a cargo aircraft at RAF Brüggen to an RAF base in the UK where it could then be unloaded without any detection.

George Stewart knew that there were several ways this could be done, and he thought about packing the cocaine in amongst parts consignments or sending it in personal parcels on an RAF scheduled flights to other bases, but these methods involved several variables. Parts consignments could be opened by the wrong airmen or the crates carrying the parts could be damaged during unloading. Even though this was a rare occurrence, it had happened on a few occasions. In addition, parcels could go astray or be accidentally sent to the wrong base.

The RAF was an efficient organisation, but it wasn't The Royal Mail and even they had the occasional mishap. In the end, the answer he decided on was for them to travel on the flight and carry the drugs personally to hand over to another member of the team in the UK. This to George was the best and simplest way to transport the cocaine without detection. A personal holdall was allowed to be taken by the NCO accompanying the supply flights. The flights themselves could be sent to any RAF base to supply or collect a specific part or parts with authorisation by a senior officer.

The first part of the plan was to be assigned to a specific flight and the second and more important part of the plan was to board the flight after any pre-flight checks had been completed. Senior NCOs were usually one of the last people to board before take-off and no one dared to check their own personal luggage. They were senior non-commissioned officers and to challenge them in any way could turn out to be a very bad move as your life as a junior airman could be made very uncomfortable on the base after such an incident.

George could move from Brüggen to any base in the UK with relative ease. If the NCO at the flight destination in the UK at the RAF base was assigned to do the checks on the incoming flight and they were of a junior rank known to George, then Sergeant Mark Watton would never have to suffer the indignity of a personal check. The genius of the system was to make sure that they were always assigned to check each other's flights on arrivals and departure times. They also did the customs checks and flight searches too and this was also strictly controlled by them.

If the two senior NCOs needed to be periodically assigned or seconded to bases in the UK or abroad for a week or so, they would be assigned to train junior ranking airmen in the art of transportation, supply and logistics at any of the bases they sent themselves to. All they needed was a senior officer to authorise and sign the requests as well as issuing the order for the men to be sent on training assignments; this proved to be the master stroke of their plans. In the RAF, orders issued by senior officers are carried out to the letter without any questions by any junior ranks.

In the transport and logistical world, RAF Squadron Leader David Walker's orders were never challenged. While George was seconded to other bases it was also arranged for him to meet either Sergeant Mark Watton or Chief Petty Officer Paul Wilson at pre-arranged locations and times. He would then pass the cocaine to them for their safekeeping until George could arrange the collection and the distribution and payment, which was done on his frequent visits when he was on leave. None of his leave would be written in his files and his colleagues at RAF Brüggen thought he was on another training trip. For this reason, George delegated a lot of his own tasks on the base but made sure they were all completed in his name and all to the highest standards. George ran a very tight section and the men serving under him would all testify to that.

As long as they didn't get careless or greedy and did not draw attention to themselves, or to any of the flights they assigned themselves to, it was a fool proof way of smuggling the drugs and would continue to be unhindered or questioned. It was decided by all four men that they would never do more than two drug runs per month, with a maximum load of ten kilos and if it was even slightly suspect, a run would be called off. It was still a very dangerous proposition for the four men, a proposition that was netting them millions of pounds in profit but was very difficult to keep secret at the distribution end. George had struck a deal that allowed the cocaine to be sold at eighty-five per cent pure and under market value in the UK but the quantities being brought in by the military smuggling ring was beginning to destabilise the market and this was arousing suspicion by the people they sold it on to. For this reason, they decided on stopping after reaching the agreed two-year target time, no matter what. They had just a few months left to reach this agreed time and stop completely but David Walker was the only one who didn't want to stop now. This was the first time in years that he hadn't felt under terrible financial pressure and was able to sleep soundly, thanks mainly to the spending habits of his demanding and greedy wife. All four men had earned a vast amount of money: a sum of money way beyond their wildest expectations from their drug-smuggling operation.

George now felt that they were pushing the envelope and their luck could run out at any moment. The operation was run as a business and George had already decided to call a meeting, an "extraordinary general meeting" to put the idea of stopping early to the other three men, and all getting out while they could enjoy the money they had all made.

Chapter 7
The Chameleon

The chameleon was a perfect way to describe Mickey Ryder. The chameleon could change colour and blend in with its surroundings whilst still having the ability to strike with lightning speed at its prey.

Michael Ryder or 'Mickey' as he liked to be called by his associates had the outward appearance of an easy-going affable man. He was the kind of man who could put a person at ease within minutes of meeting them. His light mood and good sense of humour made people relax and like him instantly, but he did not allow anyone to get close enough to get to know the real Michael Ryder. This was why he had no real friends, just acquaintances. Mickey was the middleman; he put certain people in touch with other people to do deals, and this was for a very large commission. What he did would normally involve drugs, but he had been known to dabble in deals involving counterfeit money, money laundering, bearer bonds and even smuggled gold bullion on one occasion. Mickey Ryder would put people together and deal in anything that was profitable to him. He had been introduced to George Stewart by an old school friend and mutual acquaintance, police Inspector Simon Marshall. Inspector Marshall was paid a monthly cut of ten thousand pounds of the profits from the smuggling ring and George was more than happy to pay this monthly fee to him for three reasons. The first reason was that George would not have been able to find a man like Mickey Ryder himself as the world Mickey moved in was far removed from the world George, as a military man, was used to. Even when George was home on leave, he didn't move in the same circles. Secondly, the inspector could be useful and used for information, for example, if the Merseyside police were asking questions regarding any of their deals. The third and most important reason was that it ensured the inspector's silence if he himself was being paid from the profit, he would not want to chance helping with their capture and by doing so by possibly incriminating himself in the deals.

George looked at Simon Marshall as a necessary expense; he wasn't at all surprised that as a police inspector he knew and could recommend a man like Mickey Ryder. He, like many others who knew Simon Marshall, had rightly suspected that he was a less-than-honest policeman and was 'on the take' as it was called in the criminal world, due to his general demeanour and lifestyle choices.

Simon Marshall lived in a large house and liked nice holidays. He drove an expensive car, and these were all things that an honest policeman on his salary couldn't really afford.

This was the main reason he had decided to meet with Simon Marshall and then tentatively broach the hypothetical subject of finding a man who could quietly dispose of regular quantities of cocaine in return for a large monthly fee to be paid to him in cash. Simon had pretended to be shocked and affronted at first, even to be asked such a question before subtly asking how much he would benefit per month if he did happen to know someone and eventually recommending Mickey.

George had decided to pay Mickey Ryder above his normal rate as he wanted Mickey to sell the cocaine as his own and not as a middleman. Lastly, he wanted to ensure that none of George's details would be known to the men Mickey sold the cocaine to. Men like Callum O'Neil, who was a high-profile underworld figure whose network of contacts was thought to spread across Europe. O'Neil had already served time for a plot to smuggle ecstasy tablets into the UK from Belgium. He had been arrested in a side street in the Belgium town of Tongeren after he and his associate, Craig Murray, were spotted handing over a black holdall to Victor Roneck and Alex Mertens who were in a van at the time. Belgian police moved in on the group, arresting O'Neil and Murray at the scene. They found Roneck and Mertens with the bag inside the van. The bag was found to be empty, but 14 kilos of ecstasy tablets were found hidden beneath a false floor in the van. His arrest led to a series of other raids in the UK by the National Crime Agency. Text messages and notes written down on scraps of paper led to four other men involved in the plot being arrested in St Helens and Cheshire. This was exactly the kind of man that George Stewart wanted to avoid dealing with personally, so it was agreed that Mickey would front all of the deals. For doing this Mickey was paid a cut instead of a percentage. The ability for Mickey Ryder to make everyone large amounts of money for those he did business with. This meant his services were always in high demand and he seemed to have the 'Midas touch'. This was a winning formula to be able to make many thousands of pounds for himself and for those he set up the deals with. For this reason, the nickname he was jokingly called, amongst the criminal fraternity was 'The Grand Master', because he made 'grands' for those he worked with.

George had been extremely cautious when setting up how he would do business with Mickey, and to ensure that the money never changed hands between them. Mickey would set up the deals then different times and locations were picked by George. He would then drop off the kilos of cocaine in a rucksack at his pre-arranged location and watch Mickey collect the rucksack from a safe distance through a pair of powerful Karl Zeiss RAF issue binoculars. Once Mickey had completed the deal, the money minus his agreed cut would be paid into a bank account in the Isle of Man, which was set up by George. It was a real business account set up in false names for such transactions. The funds in this account were quickly transferred to other offshore accounts and dispersed again to numbered Swiss bank accounts.

George knew that the secret to a successful drug-smuggling operation was to think like an accountant; whilst this system he had designed was to make the money hard to trace, he knew it was in no way infallible. It did prevent the transactions from being linked directly back to him and the others, although he wasn't familiar with the world that Mickey and his associates moved in. He was taking every precaution to prevent that world and the police from coming to him.

Mickey Ryder was an enigma and although he could appear to be friendly, charming, and funny, George was a very good judge of character, and he knew it was all an illusion. Any man who survived and prospered in Mickey's line of work had to be cold and calculating as well as a shrewd businessman when required. The men Mickey dealt with respected him to some degree but also feared him, but the fear was more about who he had a connection with rather than fearing Mickey himself.

He was seen by his associates and peers as a man who had a certain style as well as a lot of nerve and bottle. The men Mickey dealt with could never really work him out but as long as he continued to make large amounts of money for them, they didn't care, and they left him to do what he was good at.

It would, however, occasionally arouse some suspicion when the police arrested someone with whom he had done business in the past, but this was mostly put down to being an occupational hazard in the line of business they were all involved in.

Mickey always appeared to be interested and genuinely the kind of man who would go out of his way to help a new contact, but this was feigned interest usually to build up their trust. He would eventually work out a way of using new contacts for his personal gain. If they could not offer him some gain or advantage, he lost interest in them rapidly. He never let anyone get too close or get to know his real personality.

On the outside, Mickey was a very likeable man with a lot of endearing traits, but he was not a man to take lightly. He could also be a very dangerous man to know if you happened to be one of his unfortunate criminal associates on the edge of his world. For some reason, these men seemed to get arrested and quickly drop off the scene as quickly as they appeared.

Mickey Ryder spent his time living in two cities: Liverpool and Sydney in Australia. He had spent time as a young man in the Merchant Navy and had on one occasion jumped ship in Sydney. Jumping ship was a term used for staying in a particular port as your ship sailed and eventually working your passage home on another merchant ship that came into port at a later date.

Jumping ship was frowned upon by the ships' officers but reluctantly permitted as it couldn't really be stopped. It did stop you from gaining any kind of rank or position on merchant ships as 'jumping ship' went on sailor's records and was entered in the sailing log books that all merchant sailors were required to carry. Jumping ship made it hard to get another ship to work on but it didn't stop sailors from doing it altogether. It was while he had jumped ship in Australia, he had spent time in Bondi Beach.

During his unscheduled stopover in Sydney, he found that he loved the laid-back way of life in Australia and he liked the Aussie people. He particularly liked their attitude to their working life. They worked to live instead of living to work which was the way most Brits seemed to have to do.

Most Australians worked early in the morning when the temperature was cooler and then they relaxed with friends and family in the afternoon. He thought that this was a far more sociable and pleasant way of life and it suited him, so much so he bought a modest house there for himself. He also bought another house for his only daughter and her family when she had told him of her desire to emigrate to Australia with her husband and his only granddaughter. Both houses were bought and paid for in his daughter's name as he, like others in his profession, was very careful not to accrue assets in his own name, due to the proceeds-of-crime laws in both Britain and Australia.

Mickey had two broken marriages and divorces behind him which was par for the course in his line of work. He made sure that his daughter and her family wanted for nothing financially proving that there was a softer side to him when it came to his family. With splitting his time to live in the two countries, he had become a frequent flyer and luckily, he didn't suffer badly from jet lag. Only his immediate family knew that Mickey had a home in Sydney. It was his place where he could switch off from the constant pressure of dealing with men that would sell their own mothers for money. Mickey enjoyed his life in Sydney where he could become relaxed and almost normal again. He was an extraordinary man who could appear ordinary to all. He was a 'chameleon' in every sense of the word.

Chapter 8
Sales and Distribution

George realised during the planning stage that getting the drugs into the country was just the first obstacle in an incredibly risky business. Once the cocaine had been smuggled into the country, this for him was the most dangerous part of the whole operation. For the selling and distribution, they needed a regular pipeline and, as in any business or successful enterprise, they needed a national distributor or sales manager; the difference with an illegitimate business was that they needed someone with whom they could do business while they remained anonymous.

This was complicated further by the amounts of money involved, as George also realised, in the drugs game some of the men involved would think nothing of having rival dealers eliminated.

A very cautious approach to finding the solution to this problem was required. George had not led a sheltered life; before joining the RAF, he was raised in an inner-city area and the circles that George and his three partners moved in now, were worlds away from the circles the men they were required to sell the drugs to, moved in. George had formulated a plan to ask his old school friend for help in this matter. This wasn't going to be an easy solution. The answer to the problem was his old school friend, Simon Marshall, who was a Merseyside police inspector involved in the licencing of clubs and public houses throughout the northwest.

It just so happened a meeting was about to take place between George's friend, Inspector Simon Marshall, and a man named Mickey Ryder. Neither Inspector Marshall nor George Stewart knew at this time, that this man would turn out to be the ideal UK sales and marketing manager for the smuggling operation. Mickey's underworld connections and his ability to strike a deal made him the perfect man for the job.

Inspector Marshall spent his time mostly studying CCTV or in a court arguing licencing applications and conditions. It was difficult to get some pubs and club owners to amend their ways and become law-abiding business owners as some of these same men were responsible for bringing the drugs into Merseyside in the first place. Most licensees were law-abiding and some employed security if required. In general, they ran respectable establishments but in every major city there are pubs and clubs, where no respectable people would knowingly venture into; these were the types of places where Inspector Marshall concentrated on getting the owners to act more responsibly.

Mickey Ryder had been asked by his criminal associates to approach Inspector Simon Marshall and try to persuade him to ease off from certain establishments that had already been issues with licencing warnings. He'd agreed to try to arrange this for a substantial fee, as in the world Mickey moved in, nothing was for free.

His method of approach was going to be unusual, as he planned to agree to any required measure that Simon Marshall demanded such as extra security or bounces on the doors. He was also going to suggest entry searches including handheld metal detectors for concealed weapons as well as further CCTV cameras to be installed and immediate ejections or police involvement for people caught taking or dealing drugs whilst on the premises.

These measures went further than was asked for by Inspector Marshall and although all these things meant further expenses to the owners, it was far better than closures and no income. Mickey figured that these measures would need to stay in place for six months before a gradual easing off when things had settled down. He also figured that Inspector Marshall could be very useful in helping him close down rival establishments, which would make his associate pubs and clubs substantially more profit. For this service, he could charge a decent fee which he would agree to split with the inspector. He thought to himself that if he handled this right, it could be a very lucrative proposition for all concerned. The biggest problem was how to get a Merseyside police inspector with over twenty years' service in the force to agree to help him in this criminal endeavour. As it turned out, he was worrying needlessly.

Simon Marshall agreed to meet Mickey Ryder in a small café in Bold Street, the main thoroughfare in Liverpool's city centre. He thought he was going to discuss improvement measures with one of the owners of Smokey Mo's, a bar in Liverpool since he had issued a public disorder notice only two weeks prior.

Smokey Mo's was a notorious rough house of a pub where fights and general rowdiness were commonplace. The live music and cheap beer available on weekdays as well as weekends, plus its prime location right in the centre of the city, ensured the bar remained busy to the point of being overcrowded but it remained a very profitable enterprise for its owners. The number of man-hours spent on police visits and arrests for petty offences and drunkenness meant that Inspector Marshall was under considerable pressure from his bosses to either see a big rapid improvement in behaviours of the pub's clientele or to get the court and council to agree to a closure. It was agreed by the council and the police authority that a balance was required regarding the licenced establishments in the city centre. Liverpool needed lively bars which offered a good atmosphere and live music to attract the lucrative tourist trade, just not too lively. Liverpool relied on tourists and needed to bring in revenue from tourism; the pubs and clubs were all part of attracting tourists.

Chapter 9
The Deal

Simon Marshall started the conversation, "I take it you agree with my findings regarding your pub, Mr Ryder?"

Mickey just nodded his head and said nothing; the inspector went on, "In any case, if you don't agree to implement my recommended changes and implement them quickly — in fact, implement them from today, it will be a formality to have you closed down completely. I already have the paperwork prepared and ready to submit to the court, with your recent record of your patrons fighting inside and outside of your pub on numerous occasions. It will be a formality to close you down for good!"

Mickey smiled and said, "Firstly, Inspector Marshall, thank you for taking time away from your busy schedule to meet me face to face. It is very much appreciated, and I agree with all your proposals, although I don't think they quite go far enough." This disarmed the inspector instantly and left him looking a bit bewildered.

He was expecting the usual meeting with a somewhat rough and ready type of landlord, who normally just wanted to argue with him or at least negotiate on each and every stipulation the police licencing department insisted on. Instead, he sat at the table with what seemed to him an intelligent man who was insisting that the police implement harsher sanctions on the way he ran his pub. It just didn't make any sense. Unless the threat of closing had put such fear into him that he was about to promise anything that he was asked to do, or it could be the case that they would never be implemented. Promises had been made by landlords and ultimately not carried out when the police licencing had insisted on changes; this always inevitably lead to a closure of the premises.

He listened as Mickey went on, "In addition to your proposals of changing the closing time to eleven p.m. and for extra licenced security staff to be on duty in case of trouble when the pub is open, we intend to install further CCTV cameras in the bar area and outside the pub. We will also have permanent notices displayed prominently inside and outside the pub. They will say that drug-taking will not be tolerated on the premises, and any instances of drug-taking or violence on the premises will lead to them being instantly ejected for police involvement and a lifelong ban."

"It's about time we stamped out this kind of behaviour and it was only a matter of time that your department got involved; I am personally very glad you did, Inspector. I have been resolved for quite some time to stamp out this behaviour in our pub. We want people who use our premises to do so in safety and promote our city."

Inspector Marshall thought, *"Is he speaking the truth, or does he take me for a fool?"*

The thought had hardly formulated in his head when Mickey went on: "I have already started this process and the extra CCTV is being installed as we speak, you can come and inspect the new cameras now if you want to? The extra security staff will be on duty tonight and we will start the one hour earlier closing time shutting at eleven from this evening. Earlier closing hours will remain in place for the foreseeable future or at least until you decide they can be amended to our original licenced time of closing of midnight. Hopefully, the measures we take now will lead to a marked improvement in the behaviour of those who use and frequent the pub."

Simon Marshall did not know how to react to what he had just heard; this had never happened to him before and he found himself saying, "I must say that this is a refreshing attitude, Mr Ryder, and not what I was expecting at all!"

Mickey said, "No problem, Inspector. Please call me Michael; after all, it's in all of our interest to have safe establishments operating in our city. I'm not sure if you will believe me, but I very much appreciate the difficult and thankless job that you do."

The two men arranged to meet at the same time in one week', to assess if the new measure taken at the pub were working. This was the beginning of a very unusual and eventually a very prosperous partnership for both of them.

As he left the café, Mickey thought to himself, *"How the hell am I going to tell the real owner of Smokey Mo's that he now had to install prominent signs inside and out, and he also had to close an hour earlier, starting this evening!* It was very hard to get the actual owner to agree to make him a director, albeit an unpaid director of the business name of the pub was registered under. He'd agreed to have the cameras installed and extra security before the meeting with Simon Marshall, as Mickey had convinced the owner that it was that or closure, quite right as it transpired.

Inspector Marshall wasn't a fool, and Mickey knew that his own credentials would've been police checked before even agreeing to a meeting between them. Simon Marshall was going to be a very tough hurdle to negotiate, and Mickey needed a lot more reasons to convince Inspector Marshall to join him and become one of his numerous partners.

He hadn't played his ace card yet though; he already knew what a licencing inspector's salary was and there were literally hundreds of thousands of reasons why Inspector Simon Marshall might join him!

One week later at the same arranged time of one-thirty p.m. Inspector Simon Marshall and Mickey met at the same café, and this time the inspector had arrived early. He'd already ordered a coffee and was sitting at the same corner table when Mickey got there. They greeted each other with a quick handshake and a nod and a smile. Mickey sat down at the table and ordered his usual black coffee. Again, it was Inspector Marshall who spoke first, "Good to see you again Mr Ryder."

Mickey responded, "Michael please, Inspector..."

The inspector continued, "It's early days, but all the measures that we spoke about last week seem to be in place at your pub, and they are working! "We have had no reported incidents and we will continue to monitor the situation closely."

Mickey smiled and said, "Yes it seems to be working Inspector; I appreciate your help with all of this."

Mickey had other ideas why there was no trouble, and the pub was relatively quiet: some of the pubs regular drinkers were now drinking in a rival establishment and known troublemakers had been warned off by 'enforcers'. These men were known Liverpool hard men and employed to 'deal with situations'. They carried out their work conscientiously and were generally unafraid of the consequences and were not to be messed with. Loss of trade and the many added expenses had made the real owner of the pub very unhappy and impatient to return things as they were. Mickey had pacified them by explaining it was going to be a temporary situation only for a few months until things settled down again and anyway it was preferred to the alternative, of being closed down, without the possibility of them ever being granted a new licence to trade again.

Mickey knew the last threat regarding the licence wasn't a big deal; if they wanted to open elsewhere, they would get a licence in somebody else's name, for example, a person who had an unblemished criminal record. Half of the pub- and club owners in Liverpool had already done just this.

In the café, Mickey was trying to subtly change the subject. He was getting ready to put a proposal of an altogether different kind to Inspector Simon Marshall. "Tell me, Inspector, how long have you been in the force?"

The inspector replied, "Sixteen years; why do you ask?"

Mickey had to choose his words very carefully; he carried on, saying, "I just wondered how you got to be an inspector in the police licencing department? You must be very dedicated."

Simon Marshall replied, "Hard work is how I got there Michael, bloody hard work."

Mickey noted that the inspector had used his first name to address him. *It was a start* he thought to himself.

Simon Marshall had come from a working-class family. He had left his local comprehensive school with few qualifications and had worked his way gradually up the ranks in the police force, starting as a beat PC. After an unusually long time of nine years as a local beat bobby, he was moved to the police traffic section where, after struggling through his sergeant examination papers and scraping through the tests, he had managed to gain promotion to sergeant. He'd been promoted to inspector in the police licencing section where he had worked for three years. The reason he took the job is that it came with an automatic promotion from sergeant to inspector, the lowest rank they could have while running a police section. It was mainly a desk-bound and thankless position in the police which nobody really wanted.

He was hated by the people whose establishments he was tasked to bring into line or close and derided by his colleagues as he wasn't at the cliff face of criminal policing. He was bright enough to know that he had reached the pinnacle of his police career and would probably have his current job until retirement. Some of his fellow university-educated officers were fast-tracked for promotion and the sky was the limit for them, but with his background and lack of higher education, he had reached his glass ceiling. Being an ambitious man, he resented this fact.

Mickey continued the conversation, "I thought of joining the force myself when I was younger. Is the pay good?" Inspector Marshall was feeling slightly uncomfortable but replied, "Not really, but it pays the bills."

Simon Marshall had subsidised his police pay by writing articles in the police motor club's magazine of which he was the editor. He was paid five hundred pounds for the articles every three months, paid from the civilian publishers of the magazine. He also received an authority fee of five thousand pounds a year, for allowing them to be the official publishers and to sell the advertising space in the magazines to businesses. This allowed the magazines to be printed and distributed free of charge to the police and businesses and the adverts also paid for the company wage bill and produce a modest profit for the company too. He used this money to take his wife on their annual holidays. This kind of money-making, although not illegal, was frowned upon by the police, so for that reason, he did not declare it as a separate income and had an arrangement to have his fees from the company paid into his wife's bank account, for tax reasons. Simon Marshall liked nice things and little luxuries that money could buy, but in his opinion, his salary was not overly generous.

So, what about what was going to be offered to him by Mickey, in the café? Maybe it wasn't going to be as unacceptable as Mickey was thinking it might be. This was Mickey's moment; the time had come to try to close the deal. "Look, Inspector, I've got a proposition I would like you to consider."

The inspector responded, "What kind of proposition?" Mickey pulled out of his coat pocket a folded A4 envelope which contained fifty-pound notes. "This kind," he said as he placed the envelope on the table. "There is £30,000 in the envelope and that would be just the start. What I'm proposing is a no-strings-attached business arrangement."

The inspector was not expecting what had just happened and was a little stunned. Regaining his composure, he looked at Mickey with a serious expression and told him in a quiet but commanding voice to 'take that off the table now!'. Mickey did as he was told and there was a brief awkward silence before the inspector spoke again, "Hypothetically, what would you require me to do for that envelope?"

Mickey replied, "Just your job, Inspector, nothing more." Twenty minutes later, both men left the café after a very fragile agreement had been reached, but at least it was reached.

Chapter 10
The Introduction

Danny Ambrose was a good friend of George Stewart and they had known each other from when they were teenage lads growing up in Liverpool. George was on ten days' leave in Liverpool and at a house party being held in honour of Danny's son, as it was his eighteenth birthday. He was also using his time at home trying to make some useful contacts for the operation. He knew another mutual friend would be attending the party, which was Simon Marshall, and it was him he had come to see and arrange a one-to-one meeting with. He had known Simon Marshall since they had attended the same primary school together and now George was a flight sergeant in the RAF and Simon a Merseyside police inspector who worked in the police licencing department.

Simon Marshall wasn't the most honest or hardworking policeman in the world and his few close friends were astonished that he had risen to the rank of inspector in the police force. He was always making comments to them about how he hated being in the force and the pay was not enough for what they expected him to do. Simon kept threatening to leave the police and get a high-powered business job but he never did, he just hung in there and tried to supplement his salary in other ways; ways that his few good friends, George, Danny and Robert all thought were illegal. Simon had the big house, flash car and a luxurious lifestyle and despite the fact that he was always crying poverty, he seemed to be doing very well indeed for himself on his police inspector's salary.

George was at the party for about twenty minutes when Simon arrived and said, "George Stewart! How's life in the RAF? How long are you home for this time?"

George just smiled. "You ask me the same question every time you see me, Simon. You could just say, 'it's really good to see you, George', just once when you see me. It would be good."

"Sorry George, it's a bad habit, it's really good to see you 'Fly Boy'."

Both men started laughing and their friend Danny came over to join them. Danny said, "Let's get a drink in the front room, as I can't hear myself think in here with this bloody music. I've got a decent bottle of brandy in the kitchen; I'll go and grab it, get some glasses, and meet you in there."

George and Simon made their way to the front room to wait for Danny. George closed the door behind him, and they were now both alone.

George said: "Look Simon I need to meet up with you tomorrow; I've got something I need to talk to you about." Simon looked bemused and said, "What is it, George? you haven't stolen a plane have you mate!"

George just said, "They aren't planes Simon; they are aircraft. I need your help with something. Can we meet for lunch? It will be on me of course."

Simon just smiled and commented, "It must be bloody important if you are paying for lunch. Let's say two p.m. at the Heath Hotel." And just as George said, "Okay," Danny and Robert walked into the room holding a couple of brandy glasses each and a full bottle of Courvoisier, so it was going to be a very long night.

The following day on Sunday afternoon, George was already sitting at a table nursing a tomato juice, when Simon arrived at the Heath Hotel. Both men looked a little worse for wear after their drinking session at the party. It was well after two a.m. when George left the party and got a taxi home, but he'd still woken up at six that morning, as he was on automatic pilot. This was something he'd done for many years while he was in the RAF. His drill instructor during his basic training had said something to him that he had never forgotten. It wasn't directly aimed at George; he'd addressed the whole training flight when he had said, "If you pass basic training and become an airman, you can go out and get pissed and enjoy having a drink whenever you feel the urge, but if you are not up bright-eyed and bushy-tailed the very next morning ready for your shift, you will find yourself on a charge and in the guardhouse before you can blink." This was something George had never forgotten. He wasn't a big drinker but no matter how much he drank the night before or how little sleep he'd managed to get, he was always awake early the following morning.

Simon sat down and ordered a brandy and soda. "Really Simon! After all you drank last night!"

"It's the hair of the dog, George, but only the one. It will straighten me out. Now, what's so bloody important that you couldn't discuss it in front of our friends last night?"

George was thinking of a way to broach the subject, even though he was still aware that he was about to ask a Merseyside police inspector to recommend someone to sell class 'A' drugs on his behalf. He just hoped that he was right about Simon; having someone in the police for information was worth the risk and George knew Simon would know the right man to sell the cocaine to discreetly for them. But would Simon be prepared to get involved with drug smuggling for money? He had already decided to offer Simon a suitable monthly cash incentive, but he was taking a big chance just asking for his help. If Simon refused to help, then the whole operation could be compromised.

George took a big breath. "I need your help to find a distributor, Simon."

"A distributor for what exactly, George?"

"Cocaine, Simon. "Large amounts of cocaine."

Simon took a large mouthful of his brandy "Are you serious George; you do know what my job is, don't you?" "Yes, I know what your job is, Simon. I also know that, like me, what you earn is not enough to get us the things we deserve in life."

"Fuck me, George, I'm all for earning an extra few quid, but drugs are a no-no. I can't get involved."

George thought it was time to put his cards on the table. "Just hear me out Simon, I'm not asking you to do anything illegal personally. I intend to pay you twenty thousand pounds every month in cash. Call it a consultancy fee if you like. I have a fool proof way to get the cocaine into the country, but I need someone to sell it, and I know you will know just the right man."

Simon ordered another brandy and soda as he had drained his first one. "You've already involved me in something illegal George, just by having this conversation."

George replied, "I know Simon, but all I need from you is to set up a meeting with the right man who has the contacts to sell the cocaine on. We have been friends all of our lives Simon and I promise you, you will not be asked to get involved any further than a recommendation. The extra twenty thousand pounds a month can improve your prospects no end."

There was a short silence before Inspector Simon Marshall said, "I might know a man George, but if I set up the meeting, that's it, nothing else. And I'd want the first twenty thousand upfront. You'd better keep my name from anyone else involved."

George just said, "Okay Simon that's a done deal. Now I did say this lunch was on me, so let's order."

After the conversation they'd had, Simon Marshall was now starting to wonder if he'd sobered up from the night before. Both men ordered their food, and the waiter left the table before Simon continued, "Fucking hell, George, I can't believe we're even having this conversation."

George was now sure that Simon was on board. "I'm coming out of the RAF very soon Simon and I'm not coming out without a pot to piss in. I want to retire in luxury, so I'm going to do whatever I have to, to make it happen. Let's talk about the contact of yours."

Simon screwed his face up and said, "He's not a friend George; he's somebody who I met through work."

"What do you mean through work? He's not in the police, is he?"

"Of course not; he owns pubs, and he definitely has the kind of contact you are talking about."

George replied "That's good. What's his name and when can you set up a meeting? I'm home on leave now and the clock is ticking."

"His name is Mickey Ryder. I'm surprised you haven't

heard of him already. He's the man who can move the drugs on for you. It's a cutthroat world you are asking me to get involved in, George."

"I know, Simon, I was brought up in Liverpool too you know and I've a good idea how this all works."

"Good, well that will be the full extent of my involvement George and I want that twenty grand before you go back, is that understood?"

"Perfectly, Simon. I'll meet you with your money, as long as this is the man that can move the product."

Simon Marshall agreed to set up a meeting between George and Mickey Ryder in Liverpool city centre the following day and before both men left the hotel, his parting shot was, "Remember George this is just an introduction; after that, you are on your own with this."

George just nodded and said, "I'll keep you completely out of this, Simon."

Simon replied, "You just focus on the twenty thousand a month George. Tell everyone only what they need to know and don't trust any of the bastards!"

It was in a small coffee shop in Duke Street in Liverpool City Centre that George Stewart and Mickey Ryder met for the first time. George was sitting at a table to the rear of the shop where their conversation could not be overheard. He had a cup of coffee and was pretending to read a newspaper. As usual, he had arrived twenty minutes early for their arranged Monday morning meeting at eleven. He had Mickey's description from when Simon had called him to confirm the meeting and he recognised him instantly as he entered the shop.

"You must be George," Mickey said as he sat down at the table. He was already scanning the room.

"Yes, I'm George, Mickey, and I'm here alone. I'm sure Simon has given you a brief outline of what I need. Firstly, before you ask, I'm not a policeman, and this is a genuine business opportunity for both of us to make a great deal of money. Simon has assured me you are the man I need, and I am sure he has vouched for me."

Mickey Ryder quietly laughed and said, "He told me you are very direct, George."

"Oh, right and what else did he tell you?"

"Just, that you would get straight to the point," Mickey said. "He wasn't wrong about that, was he, George!"

"Before we discuss business, do you trust Simon? He is a policeman, after all, a bent policeman, but still a policeman."

George felt uncomfortable talking about Simon to Mickey as he was a stranger to George. But he knew he needed someone in place quickly with the right contacts to make the whole operation work. And at some point, they needed to build up trust with each other. He went on, "I've known Simon for a long time, and I've also known he was on the make for himself for a very long time. That's why I asked him to recommend someone like you, Mickey."

Mickey was sizing up George all of the time, he was talking and when George stopped talking, he said, "Okay George, I already know you are not the usual type to do drug deals, so what exactly is it that you want from me?"

"I want you to distribute our eighty-five per cent pure cocaine in large quantities, and I want you to do this while keeping me totally anonymous to your buyers. "Of course, I'm prepared to pay you well above the going rate for this, but first I need to know if you have the contacts who can distribute large quantities of cocaine regularly. And the most important thing I need to know is, do you have the contacts with enough money to pay me regularly and on time?"

Mickey was taken aback by George's frankness yet again, at which he started to smile and shook his head. "No one has a regular supply of eighty-five per cent coke to sell here, George."

"I do Mickey and I need a man I can trust to do it. Are you that man?"

"Yes George, if what you are saying is true, I could be that man. I would need samples to show my prospective buyers." George just smiled at what Mickey had just said to him as he answered, "I've already anticipated that and there's a kilo of the product in that small black canvas bag under the table. Give me your phone number and I will text you the bank account details that I want the sixty thousand pounds paid into. In future, I will want seventy thousand a kilo. At eighty-five per cent pure coke, I'm sure you will earn a healthy amount of profit. If this deal goes ahead without any problem, we can talk about making you a partner in the future. Consider this kilo a test run."

Mickey Ryder, to his credit, didn't flinch as he said, "If this one is as pure as you are saying George, you can text me your bank account details, and I will have the money in your account by the end of the day tomorrow." He took a pen out of his coat pocket and wrote his mobile phone number on George's newspaper. He tapped the bag under the table lightly with his foot and said, "One final question George: if this turns out to be what you say it is, how many more of these can you supply a month?"

George smiled and said "You just might be the man I'm looking for after all, Mickey. How many can you realistically handle? I can supply you with lots of those each month."

Both men smiled at each other and Mickey said, "This is

going to be a very profitable business for both of us, George."
"Text me the number of your account details within the hour."

With that, Mickey shook George's hand, picked up the small black canvas bag at his feet and got up from the table. While still scanning the room like a hawk, he made his way to the door and left the coffee shop.

George had a gut feeling that Mickey was the right man to sell and distribute the cocaine. However, until that first payment was paid into their bank account, which was opened specifically for this purpose, it was all still in the lap of the gods, he thought to himself. George finished his coffee and picked up the newspaper with Mickey's mobile number written on it, which he would text shortly with the bank account details. There was nothing more for George to do now but wait for the following day.

George checked the bank account the next day and the sixty thousand pounds had been deposited just as Mickey had said it would be. George had bought a burner mobile phone and rang the number Mickey had given him and to his surprise, Mickey answered, "Hello George I've been waiting for your call; I take it you have got the money?"

"Yes, Mickey I have, I'm surprised you have given me your personal phone number."

"I gave you one of my phone numbers George, and as you said we need to trust each other from the very start. By the way, your coke turned out to be eighty-seven per cent pure not eighty-five! So we are in business, George. I will take up to ten kilos at a time at the seventy thousand a kilo we agreed." George replied, "Okay Mickey, I've got another seven kilos you can have now. Let's meet up again at Calderstones Park Café to iron out the details. And Mickey, come in your car this time, as I will have a slightly bigger holdall with me!"

Chapter 11
The Naval Connection

The only navy serviceman involved in the operation was Chief Petty Officer Paul Wilson, who was a highly intelligent man. He had served sixteen years in the Royal Navy. On first joining the Royal Navy he had originally trained to be a hydrographical surveyor, which job involved surveying the sea floor of harbours and ports looking for wreck hazards or large rocks that could hamper ships entering or leaving ports. It was a complicated job that was done to keep the Royal Navy transportation system moving.

He was seconded to the supply section as cover for a couple of weeks and he found he had a natural aptitude for logistical organisation and he liked the work, so he remustered, meaning he transferred to the Royal Navy Supply and Logistics section. Paul Wilson was a big man and stood at six feet two inches in height. He had piercing blue eyes which seemed to look straight through you. He had light brown fair hair with a full beard and moustache, which had a touch of ginger in it, and when he spoke, people tended to listen. It had taken him fourteen years to reach the rank of Chief Petty Officer, which he'd held for two years after he'd served six years as a Petty Officer First Class.

During his time in the Royal Navy, he'd seen active service and had come under fire on a couple of occasions, once by Somalian pirates whilst rescuing a Spanish fishing vessel in the Indian Ocean off the coast of Somalia. When asked by his friends and family about the time he'd come under fire during his active service he would say, "It was in the small print of my contract when I joined up!" and make light of his experiences. That was just the kind of man he was.

His job as a supply officer meant he was in charge of stocktaking the stores on the base as well as being in charge of the supply chain on board the Royal Navy ships that were docked. He'd been seconded to customs and excise on several occasions for training and this was to prove a valuable experience to him and the organisation. Chief Petty Officer Wilson had an air of quiet authority about him, and his orders were never questioned. His good sense of humour ensured he was popular and well-liked by all his comrades. He was looked upon as a first-rate non-commissioned officer and none of his colleagues had any suspicions of his involvement with a drug-smuggling operation. He'd met George Stewart on a joint services parachute course that they'd both attended in Lippspringe army base in Germany. Both were young men a few years into their military careers. George Stewart has signed up for the two-week course as he'd seen it advertised in the station orders and he wanted to get a set of wings to put on the sleeve of his uniform. Paul Wilson had signed up for the course because he was an adrenaline junkie and couldn't care less about the wings. They were the only two non-army lads out of eighteen men on the course. They had stuck together mainly to get through the ribbing dished up to them daily by the army lads. The army lads on the course called them things like the 'Brylcreem paratroopers' and 'the flying sailors'; all good-natured banter. Most of the army lads secretly admired their courage for coming to an army base for the parachute course in the first place. Only twelve men out of the eighteen who started the course made it to the end and passed. You were allowed to refuse to jump only once when the aircraft was on the ground but not when it was in the air as a refusal to jump after take-off meant the man was RTU. Being 'Returned To Unit' wasn't a punishment, it was a precaution in case you scared the other men on the course and started a chain reaction of refusals. At the end of the course — and after doing two parachute jumps a day, which started on a static line and meant the parachute opened automatically by a fixed line attached to the aircraft — you went 'free fall' which meant you opened your own parachute after jumping out of the aircraft. Both George Stewart and Paul Wilson were among the twelve who passed. Both men had achieved ten static line and four free-fall jumps. The landing could be more hazardous than the parachute jump itself as many had sprained their ankles and a few had broken them too.

At the end of the course, George Stewart and Paul Wilson were friends and after returning to their respective bases, they became firm friends who regularly kept in touch. They met up for the odd weekend or family occasion and sometimes they even went on holiday together.

It was on one of those holidays in Galicia when Paul and George's involvement in the drug-smuggling ring had become a reality. Paul Wilson still couldn't believe that he had agreed to join his friend in this incredibly risky and morally wrong venture and he, like his friend George, was still wrestling with his conscience.

Owing to their time now being taken up by the operation, holidays abroad together were now off the agenda, but they still met up occasionally. Both men were on one of their now less frequent weekend trips away to London and it was in their hotel room that Paul brought the subject up of the smuggling ring.

"I still can't believe we are smuggling drugs mate, even if we are making lots of money, I can't get my head around what we are doing, can you?"

The two men were getting ready for a night on the town and George was having none of this conversation.

"Bloody hell, Paul, we're not getting into this subject now, are we! It's not often we can now meet up for a weekend away mate, and especially with the extra travelling and workload. I don't want to spoil our weekend talking about that. Let's just get out and have a few drinks and a good few laughs. I'm sick of all the seriousness, and I don't want another attack on our moral responsibilities by you this weekend. Let's just take a couple of days off from all of the problems and stress and just enjoy ourselves."

Paul just wouldn't let it go. "Yes, I want to do that but it's just mind-blowing to think what we now both are wrapped up in."

George was shaking his head as he said, "Look, Paul, you're not the only one who beats himself up about what we are doing, but we are in it now mate and there's no turning back. If everything goes as planned, we will both come out rich men in a very short space of time, and enough to do what we both want. After all, we got involved for the money. Right if you are now satisfied, can please drop the subject and start enjoying our weekend now!"

Paul Wilson just sighed and said, "Yes okay, let's get this weekend started." Smiling, he added, "It's usually you who is the miserable bastard anyway."

He was trying to lighten the mood but deep down he knew it was too late and George was right as they were both in it for the money. He wasn't exactly complaining about what his share of the drug-smuggling money was going to be and what it would allow him to do after leaving the navy; how else was he going to afford that sailing boat?

At the time Paul Wilson was earning £45,000 a year, which was a decent salary. There wasn't any noble reason for Paul Wilson's involvement. He got involved because his friend George asked him to, and so he did. He got involved because of the temptation of money and greed. His job lent itself perfectly to being part of the smuggling operation. He was able to move from military ports in the UK and abroad at will. His orders for secondment on training exercises were signed without hesitation by his immediate bosses as they thought it was invaluable training for other seamen by one of their senior non-commissioned officers. Training would be utilised at the base he was on at the time. It was the perfect cover for him to meet with the men who supplied the drugs to them as well as organising shipments.

Paul Wilson's rank as a Royal Navy Chief Petty Officer in logistics coupled with his ability to organise his own regular two-week training secondments to the NATO Naval Logistical base of NAVSTA Rota in Southern Spain meant that with him being part of the military drug-smuggling organisation, they now had two different ways of bringing in their cocaine undetected to the UK

Chief Petty Officer Wilson would get himself seconded to this NATO Spanish and American run base in Southern Spain every couple of months for a two-week training period. He had set up a regular logistics training course for members of NATO navy personnel to allow himself these regular trips to Spain. While on these training courses, which were mainly attended by American and Spanish naval personnel, he was housed on the base at the navy lodge during the course. He was of course allowed time off from NAVSTA Rota base to explore the local region of Cadiz in the evenings and on weekends. During his time off, he would explore the locality, he would arrange to meet up with either Jorgé or Rodrigo somewhere near to the base, normally on his last night before returning back to the UK. During these meetings he would be given the cocaine usually in the amount of no more than five kilos, which would be strapped to his body with tape and, being a senior non-commissioned officer, he had no problems getting back on to the base without getting strip-searched. The following day it would travel with him while he was being transported back to the UK on board a ship. The main and most profitable means by which brought the drugs in still remained by air on RAF transport aircraft but Paul Wilson now gave them another way to bring the drugs into the UK by ship. Neither he nor any of his personal belongings were ever searched on his re-entry back into the UK. He would travel back on a Royal Naval Ship to HMNB Devonport in Plymouth.

As a senior navy NCO, he was allocated his own small personal cabin on board on whichever naval ship he sailed back on to his return to port at Plymouth. It was a straightforward process for him to take the drugs ashore unhindered, hidden in his own personal kit bag.

Paul Wilson would periodically meet George in the UK after his successful trip to Spain to hand over the cocaine.

George would then arrange the sale and distribution in Merseyside. Both men thought that meeting up in the UK for the handover was a riskier proposition than smuggling the drugs into the UK but all precautions were taken; even their meeting points were varied.

Paul Wilson provided another important route to bring in the cocaine and although it was used every couple of months, the money it generated made it a very profitable route for all concerned in the organisation.

No one suspected his involvement with a highly successful drug-smuggling ring. He, like the other three men, occasionally wrested with his conscience but like two of the others, George Stewart and Mark Watton, he'd had enough of having no work-life balance. The Royal Navy was the same as the other services in that very rarely did he get enough time off to spend time doing the things he wanted to do. Paul Wilson was passionate about sailing; he loved sailing small boats, but it was an expensive hobby and he figured he would never have enough money on his navy salary to own his own sailing boat. He'd originally signed on to the Royal Navy for twelve years but then he'd signed for a further full twenty-two years before he would have retired, but he cared nothing for this plan now. His cut of the smuggling had already amassed him enough money to retire in luxury and he intended to buy himself out of his remaining one year and four months service in the navy, which would be at the agreed two-year date for calling a halt to the operation. It would mean him getting a substantially reduced pension and his navy colleagues and his friends would think he was mad as he was earmarked to make warrant officer before retiring. But he didn't care about any of this now as he had gained financial independence. He, like the other two, was looking forward to the end of the next eight months and then having the time and financial freedom that the operation had brought him. Just a few months from now and this would all become a reality.

The Royal Navy's mottoes are, "Work Hard and Play Hard", and "A Life without Limits". Chief Petty Officer Paul Wilson was very much looking forward to putting both those mottoes to the test.

Chapter 12
The Weak Link

Every criminal organisation is only as strong as its weakest link. This weak link will eventually draw unwanted attention as a result of their actions. Many things can bring a drug-smuggling operation down, for example, if someone in the organisation is getting too greedy or they may be unexpectedly talking about the operation to the wrong person, such as an undercover policeman. But neither of these reasons applied in this particular case. These were military men and it's hard to get close to military men unless you're in the military yourself as they tend close ranks to outsiders.

This made security in the operation just that little bit tighter. The surprising thing about the weak link in the operations case was that it was his lack of discipline that made this man a weak link. Discipline was a trait that all four men were expected to have in abundance as was used in their jobs daily by all of them.

Military men are taught to be disciplined and not to be careless as showing either of these two traits was a guaranteed path to making mistakes. In the drug-smuggling game, it only took one mistake to attract the wrong kind of attention which can bring the whole operation down.

In the military, you are expected to be disciplined and cool under pressure and all four men involved in this enterprise showed these particular qualities, on the outside. The four men had all agreed to keep expensive purchases to a minimum and not to draw attention to themselves until the organisation was dissolved and they had left the military and gone their separate ways.

There was one of the four who became a weak link, and that man was Sergeant Mark Watton. The sergeant was an occasional gambler; he'd always liked a modest flutter or wager on the horses, but he'd managed to keep his habit in control and secret. He enjoyed having a bet; it wasn't illegal, even whilst he was in the service, and he didn't see it as a problem. In addition, he'd the occasional win and his losses were moderate.

Now he had access to large sums of money from his smuggling activities, his bets became larger, and his losses began to increase. For the last two months, RAF Sergeant Mark Watton had been experiencing the worst run of bad luck in his life. He'd lost a huge sum of money by betting on horseracing and football matches and he had got himself involved with spread betting. This meant that, instead of just betting on a team winning or losing, he was betting on how many goals would be scored during a football game or how many corners would be taken. He was out of his depth with this type of betting which was why he was taking heavy losses. He continued to get the occasional winning result, but this did not offset his losses; it actually compounded the problem and encouraged him to place larger bets which inevitably led to him suffering greater losses.

The term used for this behaviour in gambling circles was 'to chase your money'," and he was certainly chasing his money. The frequency and amounts involved with the bets he was placing meant he was now placing bets of such enormity that they were not going unnoticed. He was doing the very thing that all four men had agreed not to do right at the very beginning.

Sergeant Mark Watton was starting to draw attention by depositing large sums of money and flagging up large losses in the bookmaker's accounts he had opened. This was not a good situation for anyone to be in and certainly not for an RAF sergeant who was involved in a multi-million-pound smuggling ring. When he'd applied for the accounts to be opened, all four bookmaker accounts required him to provide his identity details such as his age, ID, proof of his address and a bank account for payments. He'd taken the precaution of opening a separate bank account, which he used for gambling, but he had lost a total of £550,000 over a three-and-a-half-month period of gambling. Even though his losses were spread over the four bookmaker accounts, it was still a vast sum to lose for a rich high-rolling gambler, much less an RAF sergeant who earned on average £30,000 a year. To make matters worse, if that were possible, all four bookmakers had performed a 'soft credit check' on him at the time of his application to open the accounts. A soft credit check gave them his details but did not affect his credit rating; this had been done each time he'd opened an account with a different bookmaker. They already knew who he was and more importantly that his military pay grade could not support the amounts he was gambling with in the accounts.

One of his accounts had been temporarily suspended after a particularly large loss and he was already being suspected of criminal money laundering.

Sergeant Watton knew that it would only be a short time

before questions would be asked about how he came to have access to such large sums of money for gambling. The money involved was not going to be explained away by an inheritance from his rich uncle who had passed away recently. This was the explanation he'd formulated in his mind if asked about the money and ironically there was a slight element of truth as he'd been left twenty-five thousand pounds in his uncle's will—a sum he had lost gambling on a single football match. He knew that this story would not suffice without proof and he was in deep trouble, although he still had over two million pounds in his numbered Swiss bank account. In his mind, there were two options open to him. Option one would be to come clean about his gambling situation to the other three and see if they would or could help him by coming up with an idea to explain how he had access to the money he'd gambled. Although he had broken the rules about spending the money the four had all agreed at the start and even after what had happened, they were still his friends as well as smuggling partners. His second option was to flee to a country without an extradition treaty with the UK. His reasoning for option two was that even if it could not be proven how he had obtained the money he had gambled, in his mind he had already started the process that would lead to him being thrown out of the RAF in disgrace, with a dishonourable discharge. It was just a matter of time before it would all unravel for him, and he had to warn the others.

He thought long and hard about what to do for the best and the thought which he could not stop going over and over in his head, was that his time served in the Royal Air Force would all mean nothing. This was the one thing he felt the saddest about: that, and the thought of being on the run in a

90

foreign country for the rest of his life.

There was, however, an option three, that Sergeant Mark Watton had not considered. If he didn't run now, option three was the possibility of him being caught and going to prison for a very long time here in his own country.

Owing to the large and unusual bets that he had been placing, the bookmakers had suspected him of money laundering. He had been reported to the police and he had already come to the attention of a certain Detective Chief Inspector Philip Wright of the National Crime Agency and Border Force. The clock was already ticking!

Chapter 13
The Unravel

It came without warning when the threads of the operation quickly started to separate. It was three a.m. when the mobile phone started to vibrate in the top draw of George Stewart's bedside cabinet in his personal quarters. He was still half asleep but even in this state he already knew it was not going to be good news from a call at this time of night. He took the phone out of the drawer and answered it.

"Hello!"

The caller was brief. "George?"

"Yes," George replied, and he recognised the voice instantly but still challenged it, "is that you Mark?"

"Yes," Mark replied. "Look don't say anything and just listen, my position has been compromised! "I'm out George." George's brain went from sleepy to high alert in just seconds. He replied, "What do you mean you are out, Mark? Where are you calling from?"

Mark replied hurriedly, "Just listen, George; I haven't got much time. I mean I'm out of the RAF, out of the operation and I'm out of the country."

This time George said nothing he listened intently as Mark Watton went on, "There are no links from me to you or the other two, that's about the only thing I'm sure of. I've been careful about this. I've been an idiot George, they have got me through my fucking stupid gambling!"

This time George couldn't stay quiet, and he forced himself to try to sound calm as he spoke.

"What gambling, Mark? "What have they found? I don't understand."

The reply was instant, "Look George, I'm AWOL and I'm on my toes! I repeat that there are no links from me back to the organisation; I need to go now, mate! I'm sorry." There was a click as he replaced the receiver, and the line went dead.

Mark Watton went directly from the pay phone to his check-in desk at the airport. He was about to take a flight to Larnaca in Southern Cyprus. His plan was to cross the border into Northern Cyprus where he knew there was no extradition treaty with the UK. He wasn't quite sure how he was going to cross the border to Northern Cyprus; he would give it some thought on his flight to Larnaca.

George sat bolt upright in his bed; he was stunned by the phone call he'd just received, and his mind was racing. Senior non-commissioned officers did not go absent without leave (or AWOL) without a very good reason. Mark was a man who could handle pressure and if he had decided to run, it was because he'd no other choice. All George could think about was had Mark really covered his tracks sufficiently or were the rest of them now compromised? George had known Mark a long time; they'd both joined the RAF at the same time and had gone through basic training together at RAF Swinderby in Lincolnshire.

Mark was not a man to panic; he was a trusted friend of George's as well as being a member of the smuggling ring and George was inclined to believe him when he said there was nothing that could link him back to the operation. This gambling thing had come straight out of the blue. The worrying thing was Mark had kept that to himself and not asked for his help or advice; George wondered if there was anything else he hadn't told him about. George now had to force himself to think rationally. Mark was the kind of man and friend that George would have trusted with his life before tonight's phone call, and he'd taken the time while he was on the run to warn George of what he was doing.

It was now crystal clear that all the smuggling operations from this point were now over. As military men, they had discussed and agreed to a rapid planned shutdown and withdrawal from the smuggling operation in case of such an event. The planned shutdown needed to be quickly implemented. The first thing he needed to do was warn Paul Wilson and David Walker of Mark's situation and how this could impact them. One thing was sure he wasn't going back to sleep now. As he lay on his bed wide awake in his sleeping quarters in RAF Brüggen — a nuclear-equipped air force base — he wondered how the other two would react to the news. He planned to tell the other two at first light. He also thought of Mark and all his years of loyal and faithful service to the RAF all gone now. It was all thrown away for money and worse still was that it was he who had persuaded his good friend Mark to become involved with the smuggling in the first place.

All four men had known of the dangers involved from the outset and all of the men knew it was always going to be a very high-risk game, but the financial rewards were enormously high. However, so were the consequences of getting caught. George had explained at the very beginning that no amount of caution, strategic planning or risk assessment could

94

completely eliminate the chance of any of them being caught and this is why they had all agreed to a short period of two years before closing everything down.

He had decided to tell Squadron Leader David Walker the bad news about Mark Watton at eight when he started his morning shift in the logistics section on the base. He figured there was no point waking him and panicking him with the news of Mark going on the run at that moment. He tried to resist the urge to telephone Paul Wilson to tell him about Mark, but his mind was racing, thinking of all the possibilities now that Mark had gone on the run. Paul would have to be warned but what George would say to him without making him panic was another thing. He certainly wasn't going back to sleep now. It was six a.m. when he eventually left his quarters to make the phone call to Paul Wilson from one of the communal phone boxes on the base. He knew Paul would be waking for his shift in Devonport Naval Base in Plymouth and as George left his quarters to make his way to the phone box, he was thinking how he could break the news to Paul.

As he walked, another thought went through his head: why had he got his friend involved in drug smuggling? Then he remembered the holiday in Galicia and how it had all started, but it was too late now to have regrets, he thought to himself.

The phone only rang twice before it was answered in Paul Wilson's room, "Hello."

"Paul... it's George."

"What the hell, George! Why are you calling me on this phone?"

"It's okay mate, I'm ringing from a phone box; listen, I've got some news."

"Bloody hell, George! It can't be good news if you are calling me here at this time."

"No, it's not mate. Mark's gone on the run; I got a call from him earlier and he didn't say much just that his gambling had brought the wrong kind of attention."

Paul was starting to get the picture now. "Are the police involved?"

"Yes, I think so, and they might be investigating him for money laundering."

"Bloody hell, George! How much were his gambling debts?"

"I don't know Paul, but Mark wouldn't run if he didn't think they were on to him."

"Stupid bastard must have used the money to fund his gambling."

After pausing a few seconds to take in the devastating news about Mark, Paul Wilson said, "We need to meet up, George, to decide where we go from here."

The two men set in motion the already pre-arranged arrangements for a face-to-face meeting and to decide their next move.

They all had different reasons for becoming involved in drug smuggling but when it really came down to it, they had all got involved for the money. George knew it was his idea and his train of thought was that he was personally responsible and blamed himself for his friend Mark Watton's current situation. After the phone call, he felt an almost unbearable weight of responsibility bearing down on his shoulders. Things couldn't get any worse than right at this very moment he thought. He was wrong!

Chapter 14
Bolt or Stay

The following morning after a sleepless night, George made his way to Squadron Leader David Walker's office at the start of his shift in the supply and logistics section at RAF Brüggen. He described the disturbing phone call he'd received from Mark Watton.

"He must have thought that the police were on to him, and his time had run out."

"What if he just panicked, George, and fled too soon?"

George knew otherwise as Mark Watton wasn't a man to panic. "No, David, if Mark decided to run, it was because he had to. The police are definitely on to him. I've already warned Paul."

David was shocked but forced himself to think "What did Paul say?"

George looked out of the office window as he answered, "I explained to him that Mark had told me there was nothing to connect us to him. He said he was going to stay put for now, but he does want a face-to-face meeting with me to discuss the situation. There is something else I need to tell you, David. Paul contacted Mark directly from his living quarters a couple of times and the police might link them through the calls."

David was now drumming his fingers on his desk. He spoke his next words in a very low tone, "Is there anything that could link either of them to us here, George?"

George shook his head. "No, David, there isn't; I've been very careful when contacting the others." He went on, "There's nothing that the police can link Mark or Paul with you or me here in Brüggen. I don't think we've been compromised but we have to shut everything down and get rid of any ties to the operation immediately. We have already planned for this situation and after Mark's phone call, it's now become an absolute necessity, I think you will agree?"

David just nodded in agreement but said, "I hope you are right about Mark Watton, George."

George said "I've known Mark for many years, David, and he had never in all that time told me a lie. 'He's indeed brought this on himself by gambling with the money. But I do believe him when he told me he'd left nothing which the police could use to link him to us. He didn't have to make the call to warn us. But he did and that's good enough for me. I just hope his bold plan was a good one and he gets away. The question is what are we going to do now?"

David Walker looked directly at George and said, "We are going to stay then, George. We will shut everything down as planned and carry on with our day-to-day duties. There's nothing else to do at this point. Unless we come under direct suspicion and hear anything which results in us having to run, we stay."

George just said one word: "Agreed."

He left David Walker's office and although he had a multitude of things going through his head, he forced himself to try to look normal. He strode down the iron staircase to his men who were waiting for his instructions on the hangar floor below. It was only now that they would be forced to shut the whole smuggling operation down that George Stewart's ability to 'expect the best but plan for the worst philosophy would be severely tested.

There was a saying in the RAF which George Stewart followed to the letter, and he tried to apply it to everything he did in the services, wherever possible in his life in general. It was the five 'Ps' — Preparation Prevents Piss Poor Performance. He'd applied the five P's when at the planning stages of the smuggling operation and had a contingency plan for closing down the operation if it was ever compromised and needed to be closed down. It had been designed to close down quickly and sort of collapse in on itself, but in an orderly manner and without panic. The hardest part was to shut down, revealing as little information as possible. This was a rear-guard retreat action, putting as much false and misleading information in the path of investigating officers. He called this plan 'Operation Fire Wall'." To achieve the aims of Operation Fire Wall, it was ensured that no one in the supply chain knew the personal details of the next man they were dealing with, such as their real name or living arrangements, except the four operation members.

Every member had an alias. Transactions were paid for in cash if it was a smaller deal of fewer than five kilos. Holding accounts were used that could be closed quickly for larger deals. Money from the bigger deals was transferred into offshore accounts in false company names. These were designed to make the money trail harder to trace. George knew the money was always the first thing the police and customs officers tried to trace, as it usually led to the men at the top. Importantly all four men spent a lot of time at the start of the operation covering their own tracks in the eventuality of being investigated but also to ensure that no one in their supply line suspected that they were military men. All the carefully planned and secret measures that were taken, not only to hide their own identities, but another reason for these steps, was that no one would supply drugs to or get involved with men in the military.

Chief Petty Officer Paul Wilson had from time to time been seconded to civilian customs during his navy career. It was ironic that on secondment it was part of his job to look for smugglers, the type of criminal ruthless men in pursuit of fast riches, that he and George had now themselves become. It gave their own smuggling operation a big advantage, as through the experience of Paul Wilson they were made aware of the tactics used by joint police and military smuggling operations. They knew that long-term surveillance was used as a way of catching the men at the top and some smuggling operations would be allowed to continue their smuggling for months before a single swoop to find the top men and shut down the supply routes used by them.

Knowing these tactics and the fact that Mark Watton had now gone on the run, Paul was a very worried man. He knew that it was a distinct possibility that they could already be under police surveillance. After speaking to George, he made a tentative decision to sit tight and stay put in his job at Devonport Naval base and he'd asked for a face-to-face meeting.

For his own peace of mind, he needed to contact him one last time to get some kind of reassurance. "Hello George, it's Paul, I need to ask you a few things."

"Bloody hell, Paul! I know you're on the burner phone, but we agreed not to contact each other until the meeting. Get rid of your burner phone now and I'm doing the same with mine."

Paul was starting to get pissed off now. "Listen, George, I won't call you again and I'll get rid of this mobile, but I need answers to a couple of things, and they won't wait until the meeting."

"Okay, Paul I'm sorry I lost it for a second; what is it, mate?"

"Have you taken care of our Spanish friends on the shutdown?"

"Yes, Paul, I have sorted them, and it was the first thing I did after Mark's call."

"Nice one, George. I've shut down the shipping side."
"That's good, I thought you would. Listen Paul, we've done everything we can it's just a waiting game now. Have you made sure your money is safe?"

"Yes, George I have, the money is safe it's us I'm not sure about," was Paul's half-hearted attempt at a jokey retort. George knew exactly how Paul was feeling and tried to reassure his friend. "Listen mate, if we play it nice and calm, we will both come through this. I've set the ball in motion for our meeting. Your card is in the post."

This was a code that they had arranged at the very beginning of the organisation. "Get rid of this phone and I'll see you soon."

"Okay George," was the final thing Paul said before the call ended.

The controlled shutdown plan of the operation had now been successfully executed but George knew that no plan however good was fool proof. He had gone over the details many times trying to think if there were any loose ends, he had overlooked that could lead a police investigation to them, but he could think of none.

At this particular moment, he doubted his decision not to run, himself. There was one thing he had decided to do, just in case the worst happened, he had decided to give his brother Alan a call.

He made the call to his brother in Liverpool. "Hi, Al, its George."

"Bloody hell, George! To what do I owe the honour bro! Is everything all right?"

"Yes Al, I just need you to do me a small favour."

Al said, "Okay what is it?"

"I need you to act as my power of attorney."

"Power of attorney? Why?"

"It's just a precaution, Al. It's something I should have done a long time ago."

Alan was getting a bit worried now but jokingly said, "Is there a war going on!" You're not getting posted to a war zone are you, George?"

George replied, "I'll get my solicitor to send you the paperwork for you to sign and send back to him. Then all my worldly goods are all yours, Al."

Alan said, "Okay, if that's what you want, bro. When are you next home?"

George ended the call by saying, "I'll be home soon and give my love to the kids. I've got to go."

As George replaced the receiver, he was thinking how his brother would react if, in the event of George's imminent capture, he received another call from George or the letter he had already lodged with his solicitor asking him to sell everything quickly and divide the money between his family or even if he would have time to do it. It was all part of his philosophy of 'expect the best but prepare for the worst'. It was madness that they had got involved in drug smuggling in the first place but on the plus side, the silver lining was that he was now a very rich man. The trick now was to remain that way, without being caught and losing everything.

Chapter 15
The Exit Strategy

Each man had his own carefully planned exit strategy and after Mark Watton went on the run, each man had to decide for himself if he should put his plan into action now. Not one of the three remaining men had expected the smuggling operation to be discovered because of one of the men's gambling addictions. Mark Watton had hidden the extent of his gambling addiction from the others, and it came as a shock to learn this was the reason he had gone on the run. Although Mark had decided to run, it was not something he would do without good reason. George believed him when Mark had said to him that nothing could be traced back to any of the other three men through him.

George had explained to all of them at the very beginning what 'the proceeds-of-crime act' meant and how the police could seize the money or assets bought with the proceeds of crime at home or abroad. Even without a conviction, the police only had to suspect the money was earned illegally to get a freezing order on an account while it was being investigated. He also stressed the importance of having a really good hiding place, in hard-to-trace different banking locations for the very large amounts of money they all made from their parts in the drug-smuggling operation. It was madness to suggest not spending the money as it was burning a hole in all of the men's pockets, but he did expect some discretion when spending it, and running massive gambling debts was not very discreet. This was all academic now; the question was should he run or stay, he thought to himself. After much deliberation, he decided to stay and front it out. If all three remaining men kept their nerve and closed the operation down, as they had pre-planned, there was still a very good chance of them staying undiscovered; it was all about keeping their nerve. George Stewart had already devised a plan to close down the operation quickly, quietly and efficiently in case one of them came under suspicion.

He knew that the police would try to trace all of them through any contact with Mark Watton, so each of the men already had prepared false travel records for themselves and his own were quietly slipped into his RAF personal records which were kept on the base.

The money would be the next thing investigated and for this stage of the plan he had designed a rapid close down of the financial side of the operation as quickly and quietly as possible. Money held in their Isle of Man offshore business accounts, which was for expenses and for buying the cocaine with, was withdrawn and the accounts, which were already prepared to close, were now closed and the business name on the accounts was dissolved.

The Swiss numbered accounts that the drugs money was paid into once a deal or delivery had been made were now emptied and quietly closed. Closing accounts quietly and transferring money to other accounts without going on record and drawing attention cost the three remaining men many thousands of pounds, which was 'hush' money to banking officials, but it was money thought of as a good investment by

George Stewart. He was trying to leave a banking closed end, an impasse for police investigators; this would make it extremely difficult to trace the money back to them.

The operation's Spanish partners were informed of the situation and all loose ends were closed from that direction. George Stewart took his own personal steps to avoid detection by transferring all the money deposited in his Swiss bank account totalling nearly four million pounds to another two offshore accounts held in the Caribbean. He had made himself aware of police financial recovery techniques for this scenario; he knew that the National Crime Agency had trained forensic accountants and financial investigators within the agency and they had specialist police officers who could gain direct access to banking institutions at home or abroad. These men were more like trained accountants than police officers and their sole job was to trace criminal money to the criminal operation ring leaders. There were now intergovernmental organisations and financial task forces in place that investigated the proceeds of money made by drug-smuggling operations like theirs.

George knew that the operation's own money trail would have to be closed down and made airtight to avoid detection and to stop their money from being seized, although some Swiss banks made it difficult for the police to obtain details knowing that the police would freeze or sequestrate the money from criminal bank accounts and diminish the bank's funds on the deposit in the process. While it was not impossible to access accounts it just took the police time. In Switzerland, the police needed to obtain a court order from a high court judge to access individual bank account details. The police had their own methods of speeding the process up; they learnt that if they made public the details of how the criminal had made their money deposited in the bank, the bank then wanted to appear not to deal with criminals and appear totally legitimate. They would try to protect their reputations and would then fully co-operate with the police. Once a court order was obtained, it meant that all of the funds in that particular account could then be traced back to the criminals and legally seized. The money, if proved to originate from the UK, would then be split equally between the National Crime Agency and the Home Office. The NCA would use their share of the money to fight crime, and this seemed like a fair way of spending the proceeds of the criminal's account. George Stewart, David Walker and Paul Wilson had different plans for their shares of the drugs money.

The banks had to be seen to comply with international law and all police requests when faced with court orders. This, even if the bank manager assured you at the time of opening the account that only you would ever have access to the account, and the money you had deposited would be untouchable. This was a lie as no bank account in the world was off-limits to any police investigation.

It was suggested by the bank manager that George could pay a considerable upfront fee at the time of opening his Swiss bank account, to have his personal history and banking details with the bank 'mislaid' in case of any future enquiries about his account. George knew it was doubtful his details would stay lost during a police investigation, but he paid the fee anyway to ensure a smooth transaction if he needed to transfer funds from the account quickly.

It was a relatively easy process to have both George Stewart and Paul Wilson's military movement records replaced. Their new movement records had already been prepared in advance and as senior non-commissioned officers, they both had easy access to their own files on the base. They left only the official secondment records in both of their respective files as these records were held at both bases but proving they were at another base at a specific date and time was now going to be near impossible to prove.

In George Stewart's case, as a senior non-commissioned officer, and with David Walker being his commanding officer, they wrote and then countersigned their own logistical and movement papers as required. It was their ease of hiding their movements coupled with knowing David Walker was in serious debt through his wife's spending that had given George Stewart the idea to involve David Walker from the start. Without his Squadron Leader covering his movements, the operation would not have been possible.

The men had now taken every possible precaution to avoid detection. It was now time for them to sit tight and appear normal in their day-to-day duties. This was not a time for acting nervously or for any knee-jerk reactions like going on the run, unless it was blindingly obvious that the game was up, and they were about to be discovered. They just needed to sit tight.

Mark was on the run. He clearly thought the police were on to him and his arrest was imminent to do so. His assurances to George in the brief phone call he'd made from the airport to say that George and the other two men were not compromised, and he'd convinced George not to panic and to stay put in his job at RAF Brüggen and ride out the storm.

Unfortunately for RAF Flight Sergeant George Stewart, RAF Squadron Leader David Walker and Royal Naval Chief Petty Officer Paul Wilson, the three remaining servicemen who had turned from brave, honest men protecting their country, into drug-smuggling criminals, their storm clouds were just on the horizon and all three men would soon find themselves in the epicentre of a super typhoon.

This was a storm that would test all three of the men's courage and resolve. They didn't know it yet, but a very dangerous and dark time lay ahead for them all. Their exit strategies would be tested to the limits!

Chapter 16
Postcards from Home

Military personnel are, in general, realists and George Stewart, David Walker and Paul Wilson all understood only too well that no matter how many precautions they had taken to close down the operation and to cover their tracks, it was impossible to plan for every eventuality. These were men who expected the best but were taught to prepare for the worst. They all knew from personal experiences that when there was the slightest possibility of things going wrong, they usually did. Irrespective of any amount of planning, the three men knew that now Mark Watton had run, it paid for each one of them to now have a personal fall-back position or an alternative plan. If they were next to be discovered, they could then pick their own ground to fight their own rear-guard retreat.

It was very difficult for any of the three men to keep a positive attitude whilst thinking of Mark on the run and being in constant readiness for their own impending disaster. None of the four men involved in the organisation was prone to knee-jerk reactions but they knew that if Mark had decided to flee, he'd had a very good reason to do so.

George Stewart was in daily contact with David Walker as they both worked together in the Transport and Logistics section based at RAF Brüggen where Squadron Leader Walker was George's boss. Both men were now on high alert with

Mark being on the run. It was decided for George to arrange a face-to-face meeting with Paul Wilson.

George had told both Paul Wilson and David Walker that even though Mark had told him personally during the brief agonising phone call there was nothing that could link Mark to the others in the operation, he still had his doubts. Mark would not have made the mistake of attracting attention to himself with his gambling if he had everything under control. It was now time to assume all three men were under suspicion and therefore possibly already under police surveillance and for them to act accordingly.

It was normal for David Walker and George Stewart to have contact as they worked in the same section. It was not the same for either of them to have regular contact with a Royal Naval Chief Petty Officer, given the circumstances. George had confirmed with David Walker that no unnecessary contact had been made between him and Mark, but he still needed to hear the same thing from Paul Wilson. Phone calls to each other were out of the question, but they did have an alternative way of contacting each other.

All four men had mobile or burner phones for contact with each other and these phones were changed regularly. George made all the men aware of police phone tapping and bugging, and that police surveillance techniques in general, had become extremely high-tech and sophisticated. It was agreed at the outset that all communication by phone to each other would be cut off completely if they or the operation were compromised.

Their solution to calling a meeting with each other without using phones was to use a very low-tech and simple method: whoever wanted a meeting would send the others a postcard from their home city. On the postcard would be typed

"Wish you were here!" then a time and date and nothing more. In George's case, he would send a postcard from Liverpool and David Walker would send one from Glasgow. Paul Wilson would send one from Bristol. Mark Watton presented a slight problem with this particular system as he came from Warrington; no one in their right mind would send someone a postcard from Warrington saying, "Wish you were here!" So, it was agreed he would send one from nearby Chester. All four men had an agreed meeting place in their cities that the others were made aware of. The time and date that had been typed on the postcards was a code for the meeting to be attended on the preceding day and hour.

They had all memorised the others agreed meeting places and the four deliberately chose busy public places where they could be in place and watch people arriving from a safe distance to ensure no one was following them. It had a look of overkill as well as being slightly paranoid to have a system like this in place just in case anything went wrong. George knew plans of this nature could make all the difference to making sure some of the men remained undetected or were given a chance to flee if any of them were in a compromised position or under police surveillance.

David Walker chose Kelvingrove Art Gallery and Museum in his home city of Glasgow for his meeting place. Paul Wilson picked The Maritime Heritage Centre at Bristol's Great Western Dock. Mark Watton decided on the popular Chester landmark of The Eastgate Clock, which was situated in a busy Chester shopping street. George Stewart chose the Queen Victoria Monument in Derby Square, a very well-known landmark in Liverpool City centre. It was here that George Stewart sat at a table upstairs by a window in the Queen's Arms pub overlooking the Queen Victoria Monument waiting for David Wilson to arrive. When the postcard arrived, Paul Stewart understood what it meant immediately and had made the preparations to travel to Liverpool discreetly.

George arrived at the Queen's Arms forty-five minutes early and ordered himself a pint he sat at a table which afforded him an unrestricted view of everyone who was moving around the Queen Victoria Monument. It was now 11.50 a.m. on a Friday morning, just ten minutes before he'd arranged to meet Paul. People were going about their daily business, and nothing seemed out of place. It turned twelve p.m., and on the dot, Paul Wilson approached the monument. George carefully watched Paul and he could see that no one was following him. He decided to wait a couple of minutes before making himself known. He knew Paul would be exactly on time as the military had drummed punctuality into all of them; in Paul's case, he was obsessive about being on time. Paul suffered from allegro phobia. This was a terrible fear of being late and it was likely caused by a traumatic event associated with being late. For example, Paul might have once been late in his younger years and that lateness had a major consequence'. George knew Paul had this unreasonable fear of being late and had tried to get him to tell him the reason for this, but Paul had responded by saying that being late had cost him the only woman he'd ever loved, and he would not talk about the subject ever again. Seeing the distress Paul was in just discussing the subject, George never brought it up every again. He just knew that he could set his watch by the time of Paul's arrival.

Chapter 17
The Closing Window

The Liverpool postcard said, "Wish you were here!" One p.m. Saturday on 1st May." Chief Petty Officer Paul Wilson had received it a week earlier. It was Friday 30th April at exactly twelve midday, to the second, when Paul Wilson approached the Queen Victoria Monument in Liverpool.

George Stewart gave it five minutes before going downstairs to the doorway of the pub and letting Paul Wilson see him. Both men were dressed in casual civilian clothes and apart from the short haircuts, they looked like two old mates meeting up for a chat and a pint. It was of course two old mates meeting up but for a very important reason. It was George who spoke first.

"You're not wearing a wire are you mate?" His opening comment was said only half-jokingly as their current situation had both men on edge, and suspicious of everything.

Paul smiled, took off the light jacket he was wearing and lifted up his t-shirt to show George he wasn't wearing a wire and said mockingly in his broad rhetoric Bristol accent, "You satisfied now!"

George smiled back and continued, "I'm sorry, mate. I took the liberty of getting you a Guinness, I'm guessing it's still your poison, right?"

"Mark running has put us all on edge. David says hi by

the way."

"These are very worrying times Paul; how are your nerves holding up?"

Paul Wilson took a long swig of his Guinness and said, "Nice to see you an all, George." He ignored the small talk and got straight to the point. "Christ! "I didn't even know he had a serious gambling problem! Did you?" George just shook his head as Paul went on, "What if he ran too soon? I've had no one sniffing around asking any questions at Devonport."

George's reply was instant, "None of us knew about Mark's gambling problem, and just because you've had no one asking any questions yet doesn't mean anything." George continued "Mark got himself in some pretty serious shit with this gambling habit of his, and we all agreed not to spend big until we were out, but before we start the blame game, I want to confess to you now, I bought myself a car with some of my money."

Paul looked at him questioningly. "What kind of car?" George replied, "The kind of car that I couldn't afford to buy on my RAF flight sergeant's salary."

Paul looked at him and said, "If it's confession time, I bought my daughter a house with some of my money." He went on, "I'm sure that money-grabbing wife of David's will have spent some of the money on her trinkets. The point is, George, we all intended to sit on the money, but we all have spent some of the money and made mistakes."

George just said, "Yes, some of us more than others. Mark's gambling debts must have been huge for him to draw attention to himself, but he may have put us all at risk! For Mark to have run, they must have already been on to him. I need to hear you tell me now, Paul, that no contact other than the burner phones was made by you and Mark?"

There was a short awkward pause before Paul Wilson spoke, "I've thought long and hard about that, George; the honest answer is, he used the phone in my quarters a couple of times."

George was taken aback by this admission. "Fuck me, Paul, if they are not on to you already, it will just be a matter of time!"

The colour was beginning to drain from Paul Wilson's face as he said, "I wasn't the only one he rang, George, he used the internal phone to call you as well."

George wanted to break the explanation gently to his friend sitting facing him in the Liverpool pub, "Look, Paul, there's no easy way to say this but one RAF Sergeant making a phone call to another RAF Sergeant on another RAF base isn't the slightest bit suspicious; this happens daily all of the time. An RAF sergeant making an internal phone call to a navy chief petty officer at Devonport Naval Base without good reason definitely *is* cause for alarm."

George continued, "My best guess is now they are investigating Mark's debts and looking into money laundering, and the fact he's now gone AWOL, you have days or at the most a week before they come after you! Your window of opportunity for running is now rapidly closing." Both men sat there not saying anything when George added, "What are you going to do, mate?"

Paul Wilson took another sip of his Guinness and said, "That's it then, I'm going on the run, George! And by the way, don't you fucking insult me by asking the question; you know I would never give any of us up, no matter what my circumstances."

George replied, "I know that mate; it's not a question I was going to ask!" Trying to lighten the mood he added, "I was going to ask you to get the next round in. But seriously mate, I'm sorry I got you involved, Paul."

Paul just smiled and said, "You've been more than a good friend to me, George; we all knew the risks as well as the rewards. Don't start beating yourself up now, trying to look for a silver lining. Life is about to get very interesting and exotic for me, so get one last round for the mate whose life you have completely fucked up!"

Paul Wilson had no idea of how little time was left for him to flee. At the same time as his meeting with George was taking place, Detective Chief Inspector Philip Wright of the National Crime Agency was already liaising with senior colleagues in the military police. Whilst gathering his team together to investigate RAF Sergeant Mark Watton's accounts and losses and where the money came from to sustain his massive losses, the chief inspector already had a pretty good idea where the money had come from. The clock was ticking, and the window was certainly closing!

Detective Chief Inspector Philip Wright was a very shrewd and intelligent man. He had the ability to put himself in the shoes of the people he was investigating. He believed that in all investigations it was the minor and sometimes overlooked details, which could lead to mistakes and the eventual downfall and arrest of the criminals he hunted.

He had risen through the ranks at a rapid rate, mainly due to his successes and arrests, whilst working on major criminal cases that involved drug smuggling and distribution on a national scale.

In nearly every case the trigger for an investigation he had been involved in, there were large amounts of money being spent or laundered and tracing the money back to the source usually led to a smuggling operation of some sort.

Drug smuggling was by far the commonest reason for large unaccounted-for sums changing hands. He already suspected this to be the case in the missing RAF Sergeant Mark Watton's case. Sergeant Watton had an unblemished and distinguished seventeen years' service in the RAF and after it had come to light that he had transferred huge sums of money to his bookmakers account to cover his losses, he had then gone AWOL. and vanished without a trace. Those were not the actions of a man who had Sergeant Watton's military record with nothing to hide.

Although he was trying to keep an open mind, DS Philip Wright thought this investigation was showing all the early signs of a man involved in a smuggling ring, who had taken flight on the discovery of his huge gambling losses. Either that or he was investigating the murder of the sergeant.

In liaisons and with the full co-operation of the military police and HMNB Devonport's Commander, James Coulthard, DCI Wright's first priority was to trace the money back to the source. If he found where the money came from, his suspicions regarding smuggling would be proven.

He was already sure that Sergeant Watton wasn't acting alone. There could be many others involved in an operation involving these sums of money and a full breakdown of all the sergeant's last known contacts and movements was already underway. In addition, he already had his men checking the sergeant's bank and phone records. No stone was going to be left unturned, and he wanted quick results. In this case, military men using their trusted positions to smuggle arms or drugs made him sick to the stomach.

Mark Watton's phone records from the telephone in his office at RAF Cosford showed nothing out of the ordinary: he'd made lots of daily internal calls to other sections on the base and external calls to other Royal Air Force bases were made mainly to confirm logistical information and legitimate personnel travel arrangements. When the phone records were checked from the phone located in his personal sleeping quarters, it was discovered he had made four phone calls to a certain Chief Petty Officer Paul Wilson. The calls had been made over fourteen months and it was quickly established that they were not known to be friends and had come from different areas of the UK and had no official business together. In addition, it was established that they had never been on a joint service course at the same time.

This started very loud alarm bells ringing to all involved in the investigation. Why would two servicemen, who had never met a senior NCO in the RAF based in the Midlands and who had gone AWOL and a chief petty officer in the Royal Navy who was based in Plymouth, be contacting each other at all? The next person of interest to the investigation had just been located. Both men had been on a criminal joint services project on their own, which was quickly starting to unravel.

Chapter 18
The Parting

As Paul Wilson and George Stewart parted from their meeting in Liverpool, neither man said it, but both men knew this was going to be the last time they would meet and speak to each other. They hugged as they parted as genuinely good friends despite what had happened. George couldn't resist his parting comment of, "I'll see you on the ground mate!"

Paul's reply was, "Yes screw me out on a left-hand thread."

It was a joke they had said to each other a number of times while they were both on their parachute course in Germany where the two men had first met. It was something that was said just before they were both about to jump out of the aircraft not knowing if their parachutes would open properly.

On the very first day of the parachute course, their jump instructor was showing their particular class of students a short film of parachute jumps going wrong, and he was explaining that they should remain calm in such an eventuality. George and Paul were sat side by side in the classroom watching this film whilst their instructor was commentating on a man in the film whose parachute hadn't opened or deployed properly as he exited the aircraft. The man's parachute was twisted and couldn't open properly, and the instructor was explaining to the class that this event was called a 'roman candle' in the parachuting world, and it was an extremely rare occurrence. He was explaining that the correct procedure if this happened to you, was to ditch your main parachute by unclipping the two Capewell clips which were located on your shoulders. These clips attached the parachute to the main harness and once you had gotten rid of your twisted parachute you could then deploy your reserve parachute which was strapped to the front of you at waist height. You deployed or opened the reserve parachute by pulling a small handle attached to the parachute, and after executing this safety manoeuvre your reserve chute would open bringing you safely down to earth with a bump!

This emergency procedure would entail the parachutist landing heavily on their arse and they would have the bruises to show for it but still be alive. The alternative to deploying your reserve parachute wasn't worth thinking about. Straight after showing the student this short film, the instructor was extolling the virtues of remaining calm during an emergency parachute failure. A bright spark on the course shouted, "What if your reserve chute doesn't open?"

Quick as a flash, George shouted out, "Then you cross your legs together."

The young army lad, who had shouted out the question, asked another, "Why?"

George then shouted back, "So they can screw you out of the ground on a left-hand thread!"

Even the instructor fell about laughing on hearing George's reply and Paul Wilson acknowledged it was the start of his and George's long friendship.

Now, this meeting in Liverpool many years later felt to both men like it was the end of that friendship. Paul Wilson had already made his mind up to go on the run before meeting up with George in Liverpool. He'd not intended returning to HMNB Devonport in Plymouth. He'd turned up at the meeting to hear what George had to say but mainly to say goodbye to a good friend.

He'd decided to avoid airports on his journey out of the country. After the meeting with George, he went directly to Lime Street Station in Liverpool, where he removed his travel bag from the storage locker where he'd placed it earlier that morning. He got on the train from Liverpool Lime Street for his two-hour-and ten-minute train journey to London Euston for the first part of his planned overland route.

On arrival at Euston Station, he took the tube to St Pancras Station where he then changed to another train for a forty-five-minute train journey to Luton Station. Luton was where he boarded a coach to Europe, and he crossed The Channel on the ferry from Dover to Dunkirk as part of his coach journey without encountering any problem at the French customs check. On clearing customs, he continued his long coach journey on to Belgrade. On arrival at Belgrade, he had now been travelling for thirty-one hours and his overland journey still wasn't finished. At Belgrade, he changed coaches yet again and took another two-hour coach journey to Podgorica in Montenegro where he finally boarded another bus for his one-and-a-half-hour journey to Budva. He was totally exhausted after his marathon overland travel and his journey deeper into Montenegro. He was so glad to be resting the night in the pretty coastal town of Budva. So far so good and the transport system seemed to run on time, and he was now in a country with no extradition treaty with the UK. All was good, he thought to himself.

George Stewart had weighed up the possibility of the

police linking himself or David Walker with either Mark Watton or Paul Wilson. Both he and Squadron Leader David Walker had decided against going on the run. They decided to stay put in the transport and logistics section of RAF Brüggen. It was too late now but he wished they'd decided on one year instead of two years before they closed down the operation.

At the planning stage, they all thought it would take at least a couple of years to make the amounts of money they all needed to buy themselves out of their remaining service years and retire comfortably. When the money came in so quickly, it took all four men by surprise, but they all found it difficult to say enough was enough and call it a day a lot sooner. Hindsight was a wonderful thing but none of the men, including Mark Watton, expected the operation to go so quickly and spectacularly wrong. He forced himself to stop thinking this way; after all, what good was it doing him? What had happened had happened and he just had to deal with it. He was just thankful that they'd all had fall-back positions in place; he wasn't to know how thankful right now, but he would know very soon.

Chapter 19
The Money Trail

Detective Chief Superintendent Philip Wright and his team had wasted no time in obtaining Mark Watton's bank account and bank records, which he had his RAF salary paid into. He had used this account regularly, and it seemed fairly normal except for one thing that stood out.

He had used his arranged overdraft facility in the account regularly for years. He usually went overdrawn by a few hundred pounds nearly every month. Eighteen months previously this had stopped, and his account had never gone into the red since then. There was a legitimate reason why this could be the case: he simply might have started spending less or he could have been budgeting his money a lot better, which would not be unusual, but the date his day-to-day account started to remain in the black corresponded with the date he started opening his first bookmaking account. Had he found a fool proof system and was winning more than he was losing? This was very unlikely, and his betting accounts did not tell that story. In fact, the hundreds of thousands of pounds he had been transferring into those same accounts and he'd lost over four months before he had gone AWOL and fled told a very different story. He'd been even more careless and panicked when losing big; he'd transferred large sums of money from an offshore account directly into his betting accounts, to offset his debts. After further exhaustive enquiries by the National Crime Agency, this offshore account led directly to his numbered Swiss account. Although they didn't have access to the details of his Swiss account it was now just a matter of time before they got it. The agency's IT department had some of the best men in the world that could follow money trails.

All of this information confirmed to Detective Chief Superintendent Wright that they were dealing with a major smuggling ring, and it was now a race to try to get to the other members of the ring, as they were now surely thinking of doing exactly what Sergeant Watton had already done. No time was wasted in contacting HMNB Devonport in Plymouth and explaining to the Base Commander, James Coulthard, that the National Crime Agency wanted to question Petty Officer Paul Wilson in connection with serious offences. Petty Officer Wilson was known to the station commander as one of his best senior NCOs stationed on the base, and Coulthard was shocked to hear such news. He immediately called for his senior military police officer, George Floyd, who was responsible for security on the base and also happened to be another chief petty officer who knew Paul Wilson well. Although Floyd tried not to show it, he was also in shock.

The three men, Detective Chief Superintendent Wright, another one of his team, Police Sergeant Brian Burrows and military police Officer Chief Petty Officer George Floyd made their way to the transport and logistics section where Chief Petty Officer Wilson's office was situated. On arrival, they were met by Paul Wilson's Senior Section Officer, Lieutenant Commander Raymond Kelley whom the station commander had rung ahead. Lieutenant Commander Kelley informed them that Paul Wilson was on three weeks' leave and had left the base the day before. They had missed him by a single day.

There are over thirty countries in the world that do not have an extradition treaty with the UK. Some of those countries are very unpleasant and violent places to live where life is cheap. Some countries are absolute paradises for a man on the run, especially for a man with a serious amount of disposable money. Paul Wilson had already set up his new life in one of those.

Six months before he was forced to go on 'the lam' — this was what the criminal fraternity called it — he had bought a small, secluded villa in the coastal town of Tivat, for this eventuality. Tivat was a pretty coastal town located on the Adriatic coastline in the Bay of Kotor.

The Republic of Montenegro is a tiny Balkan country. It was not a member of the European Union but was technically still part of Europe. It is a beautiful country filled with friendly and accommodating people. It also had a very good climate and with good food and wine, which was plentiful and readily available.

The language was hard to understand or learn to speak for an Englishman. Most people spoke Montenegrin or Serbian, but it didn't present a major problem, as most of the locals also spoke English. In addition, the euro was the official currency of Montenegro and Sterling could easily be changed in most shops and restaurants. Because a country had no extradition treaty with the UK, it did not guarantee criminals safety from prosecution or from being extradited. If they were found, they could still be extradited back to the UK to face the full consequences of their actions.

It was unusual, but in a few cases, criminals had been found hiding and they had been traded back to their country of origin and from which they had fled, for concessions with the host government's consent. Paul Wilson had at least insulated himself against this by taking the prudent steps of obtaining some paperwork as well as a Montenegro passport.

Second passports were not just for spies or fictitious characters; in some countries, they are completely legal. He had also rented a small storage shed near the marina and was planning to start a new business there as a sailmaker; he'd taken a couple of sail making courses whilst he was in the navy and really enjoyed them, so for him it was the perfect cover.

Chapter 20
The Closing Net

George Stewart had now come back from his leave. He was settling back into his job and his routine at the transport and logistics section. He'd just got into the hangar at eight a.m. when David Walker sent an airman to ask him to attend a meeting in his office. On arrival at Squadron Leader Walker's office, he closed the door behind him, and David Walker wasted no time in coming straight to the point. "George I've been told this morning that two National Crime Agency detectives have arrived on the base, and they're here to interview every NCO on Brüggen!"

George replied, "That's it then, they've found a link to us! Hang on a minute did you say *every* NCO on the base?"

David Walker nodded. "Yes, every single one."

George looked at him as if something just dawned on him. He went on, "You know what this means, don't you?"

David Walker just sat at his desk with his head in his hands and said, "It means they've found us George, and it's only a matter of time before they trace the operation back to us, which means we need to run now!"

George shook his head and said, "No it doesn't, David, it means that they're not looking for any involvement by commissioned officers like yourself, or you certainly wouldn't have been informed of their arrival and the reason why they are here. It also means they don't have any idea of who the NCOs are, or where they work on the base. If they did know, I would have already been arrested. We need to stay calm, and we can get through this without getting caught. Look, if they check my records, they will find nothing that links me with any of the shipments. The question is how have they found a link to Brüggen?"

David Walker spoke nervously, "They could be sending police to interview NCOs on every overseas RAF base in Germany."

George replied, "No, there are over fifty squadrons based in Germany; even the National Crime Agency doesn't have the manpower to interview every NCO in them. They must have something specific to Brüggen that links this base to Mark or Paul, but what? It's definitely not a phone call, as I've only ever used the burner phones, and you've never contacted them?" This was more of a question to David Walker than a statement.

David looked wounded by the implication of the question and his reply was terse. "I'm not an idiot, George, they'd be on to a phone call from an officer from here back to the UK like a flash. Of course I haven't contacted either of them."

George was deep in thought before he said, "Okay, it's not a phone call then, it's got to be something we have overlooked, David. You're not under any suspicion. Can you see if you can find anything more out? The station commander will definitely know why they are here. There are definitely two people on the base who will know exactly why the police are here at Brüggen."

David looked at George questioningly "Who?"

George answered, "Your friend Lieutenant Bobby Kenny

and Warrant Officer Mark Bonner of the Brüggen military police section. Both of these men will know why they are here. You try to get some information off Bobby Kenny, and I'll have a word with Mark Bonner. That is, after I've been interviewed by them of course."

"I assume you've been told not to say anything to me, Ian or Dave?" Ian Jeavons and Dave Whiting were the other two NCOs; both corporals worked in transport and logistics.

David Walker said, "I've been told to say nothing to anyone about why the police are here."

"Good, then we can both see if we can find out what they know and carry on our jobs as normal. By the way David, you have got your bolthole ready just in case, haven't you?"

David Walker replied, "Of course I have, as we all have prepared one just in case."

"I just hope Mark and Paul have found that their plans have worked."

"Bloody hell, George! We all knew it may come to this, but to lose our careers!"

George looked at David Walker coldly and said, "This isn't the time for feeling sorry for ourselves, David; we all knew the consequences of getting caught, and we've all made a lot of money out of the operation. If we keep our heads and stay calm, we can both get clear of this. Just do your job and find out what Bobby Kenny knows."

Three days later at three p.m., George Stewart was summoned to be interviewed at the military police compound on the base. He was shown into the warrant officer's office, where he found Inspector Paul Beard and Sergeant Carl Gleeson, who were sitting on one side of a large desk, with military police Warrant Officer Mark Bonner, whose office it was, sitting to one side. There was a single empty chair facing the front of the desk, where he was invited to sit down.

Warrant Officer Mark Bonner was first to speak "These men are both police officers from the National Crime Agency in London, George. They want to ask you some routine questions."

George noticed the small camera set up on the desk pointing at him. His response was, "Questions about what exactly? Am I in some kind of trouble?"

Inspector Beard answered his question. "Flight Sergeant George Stewart, isn't it?" He was reading from a file on the desk in front of him. It was the same file in which George and David had amended all his movements and leave orders during the last fourteen months. The inspector spoke again, "No you are not in trouble, Flight Sergeant. I'm sure you know by now we are interviewing every NCO on the base with your commanding officer's approval. We have your file, and I can confirm before we start that you are not one of the men we are looking for."

George made a mental note that he'd said 'one of the men'.

The inspector went on, "But we have to speak to every NCO, so our time with you will be very brief and we will let you get back to your duties. Just one question before you go: have you ever met or come into contact with a Sergeant Mark Watton or Chief Petty Officer Paul Wilson of the Royal Navy?"

George Stewart felt physically sick at the mention of his friends' names spoken by the police officer, but he forced himself to remain calm on the outside as he answered, "No, I don't believe I have met either of those men. What's this all about?"

Inspector Beard was quick to respond to his question. "Look, Flight Sergeant, we had already cleared you from our investigations before calling you in here, but we did have to interview all the NCOs on Brüggen. I hope you understand this, and we apologise for the intrusion on your normal duties. You can go."

George got up from the chair, nodded to Warrant Officer Mark Bonner and left the room. After George had left the room, the warrant officer said to the two police officers, "He's a good man, George."

Inspector Beard said, "His records show he was on leave at the time of the call so it's not him. How many left now Carl?"

Sergeant Gleeson replied, "Not many to go now. This has been a complete waste of time. Up to now, we can't prove any of them knew or have had contact with Mark Watton or Paul Wilson."

Inspector Paul Beard spoke next. "Unless we find something today, the Chief is going to be really disappointed about our trip to Brüggen. It's like looking for a needle in a haystack. We don't even know for sure that this was a warning call from here to Wilson!"

Both police officers looked resigned to failure in finding other members of the ring on the base and Warrant Officer Bonner offered no comfort when he said, "I think you're looking in the wrong place. Men on this base are good men and not drug smugglers. This is the Royal Air Force, gentlemen!"

Chapter 21
Civvy Street

DCS Philip Wright called his team together in the London headquarters of the NCA for a progress meeting regarding the military drug-smuggling ring. His caseload was building up and his superiors were exerting pressure on him to try to get a result on this case.

His team was assembled in the briefing room which was a frugal room compared to the oak-panelled offices contained within the old ornate building which was situated in the centre of London. It was a large, sparsely furnished room with plain white painted walls. It had a large TV monitor attached to one wall and also contained a whiteboard. In the centre of the room was a large wooden table around which the team of seven NCA officers sat.

DCS Wright sat at the head of the table with his back to the whiteboard. "Gentlemen, I've called you to this meeting to see if we are making any progress on this military smuggling ring. As you know, I've had Paul Beard and Carl Gleeson over in RAF Brüggen in West Germany. They have been interviewing all non-commissioned officers on the base, so let's start with their report." Inspector Paul Beard looked across the table at Sergeant Carl Gleeson, knowing what he was about to say next was not going to go down very well. "As you all know, the links to RAF Brüggen come by way of a phone call made to Chief Petty Officer Paul Wilson direct to his quarters at the Royal Navy base in Devonport. This man is now known to have links with RAF Sergeant Mark Watton and the military drug-smuggling ring. We now know they have both gone AWOL and are on the run. The boss thinks, and I agree with him, that they have more accomplices based at RAF Brüggen. The call was a warning call to Paul Wilson to tell him that Mark Watton was under investigation and that he had gone on the run. The problem we have is that the location the call was made from to Paul Wilson's quarters is one of four communal phone boxes on the base and this can't be traced back to any individual non-commissioned officer. Carl and I have interviewed every NCO on the base except for a corporal who is late back from a week's leave. None of them seemed even remotely suspicious or fit the MO of being drug smugglers but from their military records, we were able to narrow down the list of NCOs on the base at Brüggen from forty-five men to twenty-six possibilities. The twenty-six men were all on the base at the time of the phone call. Unfortunately, after interviewing each and every one of them, none of them stood out as suspects."

It was Sergeant Brian Burrows who interjected next. "Did you look closely at the NCO from the transport and logistics section?"

Sergeant Carl Gleeson said, "I'll answer that, Paul. Yes, we did and that was my line of thinking as well. We knew both Sergeant Mark Watton and Chief Petty Officer Paul Wilson were men who worked in these sections. We looked very closely at the men based at Brüggen and they have three NCOs on that section at the moment: a flight sergeant who was on leave at the time of the call, and two corporals, neither of whom fitted the MO of the men we are looking for. To be fair, as junior NCOs, they wouldn't really have the opportunity, or the access, needed to be involved in smuggling on the base. Everything they do is checked and counter-checked by senior officers on the base."

DCS Philip Wright was next to speak, "I know we have made progress in tracing Mark Watton's cut of the money, but Paul Wilson has been very clever with his share. I want both of these men found and brought to justice quickly. We have other crimes for us to investigate stacking up but this case sticks in my throat! These men were in trusted military positions; I want this case solved and all the men involved locked up as a deterrent to others thinking of doing the same thing. This, gentlemen, is or was a major drug supply route into our country and I want it completely stopped. We've made some progress and two of the men are now on the run but there are others involved, and I want them found. I want all of your efforts redoubled on this case as we need to have all of these men behind bars."

The superintendent knew they had missed something at Brüggen, but he just couldn't think what it was.

Detective Chief Superintendent Philip Wright was already aware that, unlikely as it seemed, Sergeant Mark Watton and Petty Officer Paul Wilson were both involved in the same smuggling ring and Paul Wilson was not coming back from his authorised three-week leave.

He and his team of eight police officers had been working on this case around the clock for weeks now but they were no nearer to figuring out how the smuggling ring worked. He suspected other military personnel were involved, but the trail from Paul Wilson to other members of the gang had gone cold.

All they had was one phone call from RAF Brüggen in Germany to Paul Wilson's private quarters, made at five a.m. and this particular call had been made from a communal phone box. RAF Brüggen was a large base, and the phone call could have been made from any serviceman on the base. What they knew for certain from Mark Watton's bank account was that these men had accrued great wealth over a very short period. To do this, large amounts of drugs had to be moved into the country and then been sold. Drug smugglers always left a trail and made mistakes that could be traced back to them. No matter how small the mistakes, they had to be found.

This particular gang of smugglers were very different from the average drug smugglers. The two men who had managed to flee were British Royal Air Force and Royal Navy Senior non-commissioned officers. He suspected that there were more members of the gang, and they were servicemen in the RAF and the navy and possibly the British Army too. The fact that these men were well-disciplined, highly trained, and in Paul Wilson's case, decorated and involved in conflicts around the world, made this case very unusual. It was surprising that men like him had taken to drug smuggling. It was unheard of and something neither he nor any of his colleagues had ever encountered during their careers.

DCS Wright was aware of the vast amounts of money involved but he couldn't help wondering how all of these men must have wrestled with their consciences to be involved with such a low enterprise especially while continuing to serve their country. They had all taken an oath to protect their country from the very men they had turned into. Money could make men turn into nasty human beings, he mused. One thing he was sure of was that the men he was now hunting were intelligent and resourceful. They would all be very difficult to track down and bring to justice. Difficult but not impossible, he thought. He'd already dispatched a two-man team to RAF Brüggen to interview all the non-commissioned officers on the base.

A huge mistake had already been made by Detective Chief Superintendent Wright and The National Crime Agency: they had correctly assumed that the gang members they were searching for were all serving British military personnel, while at the same time wrongly assuming that all the men involved were non-commissioned officers or men from lower down the ranks. No commissioned officers were under suspicion or thought to be involved at this time. After all, we were talking about British commissioned serving officers; it was out of the question that such men would be involved.

Squadron Leader David Walker had already been informed of the imminent arrival of the two crime agency detectives and that they were there to question the non-commissioned officers on the base. The need for utmost confidentiality was stressed to him, for the police to be able to do their jobs effectively.

Both David Walker and George Stewart had decided not to run; they had based their decisions on the fact that neither man had any personal contact which could be traced back to either Paul Wilson or Mark Watton. Also, there was their strong belief that if either man were caught, they would keep their mouths firmly shut. This was an unwritten agreement between them, as they were trusted friends as well as partners in crime.

Fifteen squadrons were usually deployed to RAF Brüggen at any given time; each squadron contained three NCOs which made a total of forty-five men to be interviewed by the crime agency police officers. George Stewart was one of the first of the three NCOs to be interviewed as his section of supply and logistics was the section that the two known members of the smuggling ring also worked.

Inspector Paul Beard and Sergeant Carl Gleeson of the National Crime Agency asked all the right questions during the interviews, such as known movement when off the base, lifestyles and finances; all the while, they were looking for any tell-tale reactions, but George Stewart was calm and precise with his answers while being questioned, and he was quickly discounted as a suspect. His records showed he was on a week's leave, and he was skiing in the Ardennes at the time the phone call was made from the base to Paul Wilson.

There was a corporal in the RAF regiment whose job was to guard the base who became of interest to the detectives; he'd overstayed his leave period by a couple of days. After a brief investigation, it was found he had been arrested for fighting in a bar in Berlin. This had resulted in him being locked up and delayed his return back to the base. His explanation was that he'd been delayed due to a cancelled ferry sailing and he had some car trouble, which delayed his journey back. This was accepted at the time, but he was demoted back to senior airman when the real exploits of what he had done came to light.

After three days of intensive questioning and interviews, the two Crime Agency officers returned to England, none the wiser of just who the suspect or suspects were that were involved in the smuggling ring at RAF Brüggen.

It was always part of the long-term plan for George Stewart to buy his way out of his remaining four-year period, of the twenty-two years' service that he'd signed on for. This was part of the plan even before the smuggling operation had been compromised and shut down. He'd spoken at length with David Walker. Squadron Leader Walker had decided he was going to do the full twenty-two years before retiring. It was a pity, as, before the smuggling — which now seemed such a long time ago to David Walker — he was a good officer, and he was still very good at his job. The reason he'd got himself involved with the operation was debt. Despite the large debts his wife had racked up in his name, he still needed to find more money to put both his girls through university, as well as maintaining his wife's lifestyle with the upkeep of their large house in Glasgow and their villa abroad, which he couldn't afford without his cut of the drug-smuggling proceeds. Those reasons didn't excuse his actions. He had chosen to smuggle drugs for the money he'd made over the past twenty months. He would probably make wing commander before he retired and assuming that no further evidence came to light regarding his involvement with the operation.

George Stewart himself would have made warrant officer, which was the highest non-commissioned rank you could be promoted to, if he stayed in the RAF. For his last four years, he'd already been offered a full commission when he'd attained the rank of sergeant, but he'd turned it down, as he was a working-class lad, intelligent but one of the lads and that was how he wanted to remain. No officers' mess or officers' black-tie dances for him to attend; that wasn't his style at all.

He was restless to get out of the service and now he had the money he saw no reason to alter his original plan. He'd already set the wheels in motion by submitting the required paperwork, which was countersigned and approved by his immediate boss, Squadron Leader Walker.

Officially he was applying for an honourable discharge on

medical grounds after eighteen years of distinguished service. There was some truth in this as he did have slightly raised blood pressure and this was an ailment for which an RAF doctor was already prescribing him medication.

This made his request for an early discharge a formality as all airmen had to be in A1 condition and fitness to continue to serve. It was the same RAF doctor who suggested he should consider retiring on medical grounds giving him not only the idea but the perfect reason to leave. In addition to this, he had already made it known to his family and colleagues that he wanted to leave the RAF to pursue other interests, even before the smuggling operation had gone bad. It meant he would get his wish but, in the process, receive a substantially reduced RAF pension for not reaching his twenty-two years' service. It was a very unfair system in place but at that moment, it was the least of his worries.

On his instructions, his house, car and the bulk of his furniture and portable belongings were all ready to be sold or auctioned off by his brother and the proceeds would then be split between his remaining family members. The problem for George Stewart wasn't money but the timing of his request to be discharged honourably or not.

The investigation by the National Crime Agency was still ongoing although the investigation had reached an impasse as all leads to further members of the gang had gone stone cold. To further add to The National Crime Agency and Detective Chief Superintendent Philip Wright's problems, their efforts to trace the sale of the drugs into the UK had drawn a blank. The police had nothing at all on George Stewart at this time.

Mark Watton had managed to move his money from his Swiss bank account, only a matter of days before access was granted by the Police Border Force, and Paul Wilson had still not been located. All involved were very good at hiding their tracks or as it was called in the military 'moving in an orderly manner to a fall-back position'. The case was leading nowhere for the police, and it looked like the smugglers had completely escaped being brought to justice.

George Stewart was unsure whether he was making the right decision to leave the RAF at this particular time, given that the police investigation was officially active. He wondered if he should have waited longer, possibly staying in the RAF for another year or at least until the dust settled.

He quickly put those thoughts out of his mind and tried to think rationally. He was leaving the service with a proven medical condition, and nothing could be linked to him, or the 'now' closed-down drugs operation. He felt it was right to leave now. It was a further two weeks before his discharge was approved. While he was waiting for the approval to be officially granted, he'd given some thought to what he would do when he was in Civvy Street.

He didn't need to work but he was still very cautious about how he spent his money. He had limited himself to spending just his salary, which was in his current bank account as he was trying to keep things as normal as possible, for outside appearances. Quietly he'd transferred a substantial amount into another hard-to-trace joint bank account, which had been opened some time previously in his brother's name and to which he also had access if required.

George Stewart wasn't a man to make rash decisions; he'd thought about his next move very carefully and it was now time for him to re-enter civilian life once again!

Chapter 22
The Breakthrough

Inspector Paul Beard and Sergeant Carl Gleeson of The National Crime Agency interviewed a total of forty-four non-commissioned officers based at the Royal Air Force base in Brüggen, West Germany. The forty-four consisted of every non-commissioned officer on the base including Flight Sergeant George Stewart whose records had shown he was not even on the base at the time of the phone call to Chief Petty Officer Paul Wilson made from the communal phone on the base.

The two NCA officers were assisted by a senior military police officer; they took four days in total to complete all of the interviews. At the end of this process, they had not uncovered a single piece of evidence that could link any of the non-commissioned officers on the base directly to Royal Naval Chief Petty Officer Paul Wilson. Neither of the NCA officers was looking forward to telling their superior DCS Philip Wright that their trip to RAF Brüggen had turned up no new evidence or links with the drug-smuggling ring. After their fruitless trip, the detectives reluctantly returned to the London headquarters of The National Crime Agency for debriefing.

It was during this debriefing, while Inspector Beard was explaining to the Detective Chief Superintendent that the interview had turned up nothing at all, that the DCS had an inspired brainwave as Inspector Beard spoke.

"Look, boss, we interviewed every NCO on the base and none of them knew or had any connections with Paul Wilson. A few of them did know Sergeant Mark Watton, but they knew him from legitimate RAF business or training courses. We checked everything out very thoroughly and there's still just the one direct link, and that's the phone call from the base to Paul Wilson in Devonport. You know the call was made from a communal phone box on the base and it's impossible to link the call with anyone on the base."

Detective Chief Superintendent Wright had listened patiently whilst the inspector spoke, but it was the last part of his report that suddenly gave him an idea. He knew tracing whoever made the phone call to Paul Wilson's personal quarter at the Devonport Navy Base was key to making progress on this case.

He asked the inspector, "What was the precise time of the phone call to Paul Wilson?"

The inspector replied, "Five a.m., the day after Sergeant Mark Watton went on the run, sir!"

The chief superintendent looked at his inspector and asked, "The base is covered by CCTV, right?"

The inspector said, "Yes, it's everywhere."

The detective chief superintendent was already picking the phone up to make a call to the station commander at RAF Brüggen.

After his brief phone call, the DCS looked at his inspector and said, "You and Sergeant Gleeson are going back to RAF Brüggen."

Inspector Beard looked startled by this statement and said,

"When, sir?"

The chief superintendent replied, "Right now, Paul!"

"Right now!"

It was clear to the chief superintendent that this phone call from the base to Paul Wilson was made directly after Mark Watton had fled. This was a warning phone call, whoever had made the call was a member of the drug-smuggling ring or someone who was, at the very least, involved with the smugglers. It was also clear that there was tight security on the base and this tight security was going to help them find out who made this call.

The call was made from a communal phone box on the base at five a.m. and this particular phone box was positioned outside the NAAFI Club. The NAAFI Club was located in the centre of the base, and it was one of four communal phone boxes located at various points around the base. These communal phone boxes were available for use by all ranks and usually when the airmen were off duty. Brüggen was an active nuclear base and security and secrecy was vital. All airmen on the base adhered to a strict code of secrecy regarding their particular roles on the base. Airmen were allowed to contact their friends and family back home in the UK. Privacy laws prevented personal calls made from these communal phone boxes from being recorded. This meant that finding the airman who made the warning phone call to Paul Wilson by listening to the call was impossible.

Owing to the base's proximity to Russia, on the odd occasion, the Russians would have German-speaking spies who would pretend to be aircraft enthusiasts. They would sit in their cars just a short distance from the airbase with their cameras, taking photographs of the aircraft as they took off and landed.

In reality, it was to check if there had been any recent modification to the aircraft and report back to the Russians. If they were challenged, which happened quite frequently, their paperwork would all be legitimate and in the guise of aircraft spotters, they would usually belong to a local flying club. Both sides did it and both sides knew that the other side was doing it. It was estimated that in the event of a war, and the Russians attacked the base, RAF Brüggen would have only an eighteen-hour life expectancy.

DCS Wright had realised that there was another way of finding out who made the call to Paul Wilson; the DCS explained what he wanted Inspector Beard and Sergeant Gleeson to do. A day later, they were back in RAF Brüggen and sat in the office of the head of the military police viewing the tapes of the security CCTV camera located outside the NAAFI club. The position that CCTV camera was located meant it looked at the entrance to the club but also directly past the communal telephone box inadvertently filming whoever used that particular phone box.

The National Crime Agency officers were particularly interested to see who had used the specific communal phone box at five-thirty on the morning after Sergeant Mark Watton had gone on the run. The CCTV recordings were surprisingly clear which was the result of having the latest security technology which was used on all military bases.

Twenty minutes after the officers started viewing the tapes, Inspector Paul Beard made a phone call to DCS Philip Wright.

"Boss! "We've got him!" It's Flight Sergeant George Stewart! "The tapes show his face clear as day. He's the one

145

who made the call to Paul Wilson. "The records show him on leave and off the base at the time of the call, and guess who signed his leave orders, boss? "It was Squadron Leader David Walker, his section commander!"

The DCS clenched his fist and said, "Good work Paul, don't do anything yet."

This was the news he'd been waiting for. He'd had a suspicion that commissioned officers were involved in the smuggling ring for some time now; how else were the travel orders issued and signed? *I've got you all now,* he said to himself, just like a house of cards as one fell it brought the others down too. *"They always make a mistake no matter how small,"* he thought to himself.

Flight Sergeant George Stewart's life was about to dramatically change, although he'd no idea of how dramatic this change was going to be.

The phone call to Petty Officer Paul Wilson had linked him to the smuggling ring, but it was not enough to charge him with anything just yet. As making a phone call wasn't illegal, they would need more hard evidence, but he was sure that they had found another two members of the smuggling operation.

Detective Chief Superintendent Philip Wright briefed the station commander and his two detectives that this second visit to the base to check both suspects' movements and to go back through their military files with a fine-tooth comb was to be done in absolute secrecy. He wanted as few people as possible knowing why the police had returned to the base. He already suspected other members of the smuggling ring to be on the base and he now had a very good idea of the identities of at least two of those men. This time he did not want anyone on the base getting wind of his officers' presence, as information regarding strangers on the base was quickly shared. They would not get the chance to escape now.

Only two other men apart from the station commander knew why the police officers were back for a second visit. One was the senior military police officer responsible for the station security, Flight Lieutenant Robert Kenny and the other was his second-in-command, military police Warrant Officer Mark Bonner, who had met and escorted both men at the security gate and had taken them to the military police offices located in a separate compound, within the base. It was from there that the four men checked the CCTV tapes from the camera looking towards the communal phone and it was from there that they confirmed Flight Sergeant George Stewart from transport and logistics as the man who made the five a.m. call.

The other man who was now under suspicion and firmly under the police spotlight was the Transport and Logistics Section Commander, Squadron Leader David Walker! DCS Wright was kicking himself that the investigation up to this point had ruled out commissioned officers. It made perfect sense to have someone in authority to countersign travel orders. A squadron leader was a senior officer, and few people would even question his orders.

Squadron Leader Walker was already under suspicion when George Stewart was implicated, but his involvement was confirmed to the detective on their earlier visit by stating that George Stewart was off the base on leave, skiing in the Ardennes, when the call to Paul Wilson was made and also by countersigning the order for George Stewart's leave.

It was now obvious that the squadron leader was lying and part of the smuggling ring. The police investigation now moved to a different level: both of the men's movements and financial details were finely checked over the past two years.

The records of any travel for logistical movement orders for George Stewart that were countersigned by David Walker were also carefully looked over for any irregularities.

Detective Chief Superintendent Wright knew the other two known men who had taken flight were both in transport and logistics sections in The RAF and the Royal Navy. This made perfect sense that the men he was looking at on this particular base came from the same section. He had nearly let these two slip through the net. Nearly but not quite; he now had them both but needed more evidence of the men's involvement before they could be arrested, evidence he already knew would come from their financial behaviour over the past months.

Squadron Leader David Walker had no idea he was under investigation. After George Stewart had been interviewed and quickly discounted as a suspect, he thought they were both now in the clear of any suspicion. He carried on with his daily life as normal. George Stewart was also in the same frame of mind and as he was only a week away from leaving the RAF, he was busy making preparations and getting his affairs in order.

He was about to get his wish but not exactly in the way he thought, as the police had wasted no time in investigating both men's personal background and lifestyles. It was quickly established that George Stewart had recently sold his house and belongings using his brother to act as his agent for the sales. These were not the normal actions of someone about to retire from the armed forces. More tellingly was the high-end Aston Martin car that had belonged to him and was sold on his behalf, fetching the princely sum of £195,000. When the vehicle's history was checked, it showed it had only one previous owner from new — George Stewart. It had been purchased from a high-class dealership and the money to pay for it had been transferred directly to the dealership from an offshore account registered in George Stewart's name. This was a major mistake; not only having the account registered in his name but purchasing a luxury Aston Martin car at all. This was not something that could be bought or sold unknowingly. A transaction of his nature would always leave a money trail and by giving in to the temptation of buying the car in the first place, this had led to his downfall, he simply did not earn enough money through his RAF salary to have bought and owned such a prestigious car legally.

After further investigation, George Stewart's movement records were found to be falsified and after being under constant surveillance, Flight Sergeant George Stewart and Squadron Leader David Walker were both arrested by military police within ten minutes of one another on RAF Brüggen airbase!

DCS Philip Wright from the National Crime Agency was in attendance and the two men were charged with two main offences at the time of the arrests and further charges would soon follow. The initial charges were conspiracy to import and supply controlled drugs, and money laundering. At the time of the arrests, both men knew that protesting their innocence was futile, so they both exercised their right to remain silent. Silent was how they both planned to stay. George Stewart just hoped, against the odds that, given what had happened to him and David Walker, Mark and Paul had managed to stay free. Both men were taken into custody on the base to ponder their fates and await transfer back to the UK. It would be The National Crime Agency that would prosecute them back in the UK.

Chapter 23
The Arrest

It was a pity that George Stewart had not taken his own advice; he'd constantly advised the other men not to use their shares of the proceeds to buy any high-end purchases before the operation had been completely shut down. He had not taken his own advice before he'd left the RAF for his own retirement. Buying that Aston Martin was a very big mistake. He'd only ever driven the car twice and he had no time to instruct his brother to sell it for him and distribute the money to his family as it was quickly recovered by the police as proceeds of crime. It was truly a prestigious car, but it was wrongly looked upon as a symbol of wealth and achievement by George, he was a man who came from humble beginnings and by owning the car he thought that he had finally hit the big time and made something of his life. He had made something of his life before the drug smuggling, but he hadn't realised it. His working-class background meant that everything was judged by how much its monetary value was worth. It was an inbuilt desire that was found in most working-class men to aspire to be able to buy such unimportant things.

It didn't occur to him when he bought the car that it was just another personal possession. George had a successful career in the RAF; he'd already achieved a great deal in his life. He'd dragged himself out of his working-class beginnings and had forged a successful military career, and now it was about to all come tumbling down around him, and for what? Money and greed! He knew deep down that money wouldn't bring him happiness, money and wanting to own expensive personal possessions was George's personal nemesis.

Detective Chief Superintendent Philip Wright was sitting on an RAF BAE 146 military aircraft for his one-and-a-half-hour flight from RAF Northolt to RAF Brüggen in West Germany, where he'd arranged to be present at the arrests of Flight Sergeant George Stewart and Squadron Leader David Walker. He wanted to be there and see their faces as their world collapsed. The men had chosen to make money from importing drugs into the UK notwithstanding all the misery that they had caused whilst serving their country on active military service. In DCS Wright's eyes, both men deserved everything that was coming to them. During his short flight to Brüggen, he found himself wondering why two men in their positions would throw away their long and distinguished military careers for the sake of making money. He also wondered if there were any members of the smuggling ring still at large, which members of the NCA knew nothing about at that time.

Military men were trained not to give any information during interrogations, so he didn't hold out much hope of either of the men giving up information about the other members of the smuggling ring that could be still in hiding.

He would be landing at RAF Brüggen soon and he suspected that other mistakes had been made by the men and it was just a case of following the links to discover them after the call from the communal phone box had led to these two men.

George Stewart was sitting in Squadron Leader David Walker's office explaining how the NCA inspector had told him that he had already been ruled out of the investigation and that changing his transport and home leave records in his file had worked. No one was going to doubt a senior officer such as a squadron leader who had countersigned the replaced false orders.

George's thinking was that if they stayed calm, they would be in the clear and both he and David Walker were glad that the operation had been shut down at the first hint of trouble. George was now confident that neither Mark Watton nor Paul Wilson had left anything to find that the police could use to link them personally.

It felt to him that for the very first time since Mark Watton's phone call to tell him he was going on the run, they now seemed in the clear.

Only the station commander and the military police section at RAF Brüggen were aware that the National Crime Agency Police Officers were now on the base to make the arrests of Squadron Leader David Walker and Flight Sergeant George Stewart. The military police section commander Robert Kenny had placed both men under surveillance and given his men orders to keep a discreet distance.

It was agreed that Inspector Paul Beard and Sergeant Carl Gleeson of the NCA would be making the actual arrests while their boss, DCS Philip Wright, was present and accompanied by Flight Lieutenant Kenny of the military police.

It was a typical day for Squadron Leader Walker who had been in his office since seven a.m. for his early start. He'd had his breakfast in the officers' mess at six a.m. and was now sitting at his desk on the computer organising the paperwork for an incoming flight from the UK carrying personal protection equipment. His office was situated on the second floor overlooking the hangar where the logistics section was housed. The office was accessed by a set of steel steps that led to a balcony and a small bank of three offices of which his was the largest and was situated in the middle. The two smaller officers to either side belonged to his senior NCO, George Stewart and the other office was shared by his two junior NCOs both at the rank of corporal. All three offices had doors leading to a set of fire escape doors at the rear. David Walker looked up from his desk and saw five men walking purposefully across the hangar floor towards the stairs that led to his office. He recognised the station commander and Flight Lieutenant Bobby Kenny of the military police instantly, but he didn't know the other three men who were dressed in civilian clothes. As they strode across the hangar floor, the realisation of why they were there hit him! He remained surprisingly calm considering what he knew was about to happen. He couldn't even get a warning off to George as he normally turned up for work at 7.50 a.m.

It was as though time had stood still and he just felt helpless; it seemed as though it was all happening in slow motion. A fleeting thought went through his head that he was glad they had come for him now before his section got really busy. This would mean fewer of his men would see him being arrested and he would at least retain some of his dignity. A couple of seconds later, the men entered the squadron leader's office and Inspector Paul Beard made the arrest. David Walker said nothing as he was read out his rights and as the inspector handcuffed him. The station commander asked if it was absolutely necessary to cuff him. The commander explained to the inspector that there was nowhere for him to run on the base. Inspector Beard looked across to DCS Wright who was standing there impassively.

DCS Wright was adamant, "Yes, Commander, it *is* absolutely necessary. This man is under arrest for drug smuggling. Carry on, Inspector."

DCS Wright wanted David Walker to be seen being handcuffed, arrested and taken from his section by his men who were now starting to arrive en masse for work in the section hangar.

As David Walker was led out of his office, the station commander said, "Why David? Why?"

David Walker looked at him impassively and simply replied, "I'm sorry sir!"

They led him away in handcuffs to the military police compound.

George Stewart was in the sergeants' mess finishing his breakfast before he left for work. Twenty of his fellow NCOs from the other sections sat in the same mess hall eating their breakfasts and chatting to one another. The same five men that had just arrested David Walker entered the mess. It was not normal for the station commander to enter the sergeants' mess early in the morning and even less normal for men dressed in civilian attire to enter with him. The mess hall instantly went quiet as they approached the table where the now shocked George Stewart was trying not to show he was in shock at the intrusion.

How the hell did they trace me? This was the question going through George Stewart's mind as they approached him. Inspector Paul Beard made the arrest while George Stewart's fellow sergeants looked on incredulously.

"Flight Sergeant George Stewart you are under arrest for conspiracy to supply and distribute class 'A' drugs. You do not have to say anything, but it may harm your defence if you do not mention when questioned something to which you later may reply in court. Anything you do say may be given in evidence."

George Stewart didn't say a single word; he was handcuffed and led out of the sergeants' mess in front of his peers and taken to the military police compound to wait to be questioned. As they walked him towards the military police compound, a small group of men stopped in their tracks and stared at George in his handcuffs as he walked towards the compound. The base had never known anything like it and the hot topic of conversation in all of the sections on the base was what had happened that morning.

Chapter 24
The Consequences

Both men kept their mouths firmly shut whilst being questioned and put under pressure to give details regarding the other two members of the smuggling ring. They had both been taught anti-interrogation techniques in case of them being captured in active war zones. Neither David Walker nor George Stewart would have had much to tell the police about the intended escape routes or any of the banking details relating to the RAF Sergeant Mark Watton or Naval Chief Petty Officer Paul Wilson. All four men had made their own banking arrangements and escape plans and fall-back positions without the knowledge of the others, in case of capture. it was something that the four men had agreed on at the very beginning.

Detective Chief Superintendent Philip Wright had members of the police Asset Confiscation Enforcement Department seconded to his investigation team. This unlikely but genuine-sounding department had the right men as well as the right initials to trace money gained through criminal activity. Police members of ACE were all highly trained in banking procedures and were all experts in IT and money recovery.

Whilst the three RAF men had their five Ps motto of 'preparation prevents piss poor performance', members of the police ACE team had their own version. Their version was called the four Ps (Pursue, Prepare, Protect and Prevent). These police officers were dedicated and tenacious in doing their duty.

The crack police team quickly established what Squadron Leader David Walker had done with the majority of his share of the proceeds gained from his involvement with the drug-smuggling ring. He'd deposited £500,000 in an offshore bank account which his wife had access to. She periodically transferred large sums of this money directly into her current account to fund her lavish shopping sprees. He had stupidly transferred money directly into his two daughters' bank accounts. Both of his daughters lived away from home and were at university and this, coupled with his having his money spent by his greedy social-climbing wife, was why he had agreed to get involved with the drug smuggling in the first place. The direct money transfers to each of his daughters led the police directly to his Swiss bank account which contained the bulk of his drug-smuggling proceeds.

It took the National Crime Agency a little time to get a court order to gain access to his Swiss bank account. Eventually, with the bank agreeing to co-operate fully with the police investigation, David Walker lost all of the money that both the Swiss and the other offshore accounts contained. In addition to losing the majority of the money, he also lost his villa in Portugal which was also proven to have been partly bought and paid for with the proceeds of crime. His wife was forced to sell their large house in Glasgow and downsize to a small apartment to pay their legal fees. She herself only narrowly avoided going to prison as she obviously knew the money was not coming from her husband's RAF earnings.

However, it could not be proven that she knew about her husband's involvement with the drug-smuggling ring and in exchange for David Walker and his wife both agreeing to stay silent and avoid all publicity to do with the case, his wife was spared going to prison and received a suspended sentence for being an accessory after the fact.

The newspapers were quickly on to the story after the arrests of Squadron Leader David Walker and Flight Sergeant George Stewart. It was a big story as the involvement of a fully commissioned RAF officer and his subordinate non-commissioned officer in a drug-smuggling operation was unprecedented.

The headlines on the run up to their trail read.

MILITARY GANG MEMBERS ACCUSED OF IMPORTING DRUGS WORTH MILLIONS OF POUNDS.

Suspected members of an international military gang who have smuggled multi-millions of pounds worth of drugs into the UK have been arrested at RAF Brüggen Royal Air Force Base in West Germany. It is suspected that further military bases have been used by this gang at home and abroad.

The National Crime Agency (NCA) said the scale of the gang's drugs smuggling is estimated at many millions of pounds and two men have been arrested for drug-related offences at RAF Brüggen. One of the men is believed to be a commissioned officer. They are accused of being part of an organised crime group that imported large amounts of cocaine into Britain using military air and sea transport.

The NCA said it was unprecedented that a senior commissioned officer and his subordinate non-commissioned officer are involved in drug importation and distribution throughout the UK. It is believed that a further two known military suspects are being hunted due to their involvement with the drug-smuggling operation and it is suspected that further accomplices remain undetected in the NCA ongoing investigation. The drugs are believed to have been brought into the UK through British Air Force bases and Naval ports over an eighteen-month period. An investigator revealed that the same group had made numerous successful imports resulting in large amounts of cocaine being distributed throughout the UK.

Chief Superintendent Philip Wright, the NCA Regional Head of Investigations, said, "This unprecedented group of military officers fuelled a drugs trade that has been linked to rising violence. Stopping criminals who don't care about the damage they are causing in communities is an absolute priority. We suspect that these men were involved in a large-scale operation bringing in many kilos of cocaine that were distributed to crime groups throughout the UK. By working closely with our police and military partners here and overseas, we believe we have dismantled a well-established drug supply route."

The tabloid papers were offering large sums of money for his wife's side of the story; after all, it was unprecedented that a senior high-ranking RAF commissioned officer had got caught up in a seedy drug-smuggling ring whilst serving at a high-security RAF base. It was believed wrongly that because of his rank as a senior commissioned officer that Squadron Leader David Walker was the mastermind and ringleader of the drug-smuggling ring. For this reason, he was sentenced to an eighteen-year prison sentence. He was stripped of his commission, dishonourably discharged from the RAF and his name was struck from his squadron records. The honourable

Mr Justice Houseman said during his sentencing at the trial that David Walker was a disgrace to his commission, the Royal Air Force and the men who had served under him. It was only his long service record and the fact that he had served with some distinction on active service that had prevented him from receiving a substantially longer sentence.

Flight Sergeant George Stewart received a fourteen-year sentence along with a dishonourable discharge but although the police tried extremely hard, to locate the money he'd made from being involved with the drug-smuggling ring, it could not be found. He repeatedly refused a shorter sentence plea deal to disclose where he'd moved his money. The police threatened to prosecute his brother as an accessory after the fact unless George Stewart told them where his money was hidden, but this fell on deaf ears. Eventually, with insufficient proof, this avenue of the investigation came to nothing as George knew it would. He'd done a very good job of closing the financial door to the police on where he had hidden his share of the money.

George Stewart had always been a man who hoped for the best but expected the worst. His reasoning was now he'd been captured his career was already ruined and giving the money up to the police would not change this. He had secretly instructed a lawyer to have papers drawn up which gave his brother power of attorney and access to all George Stewart's known assets.

It was a simple step to let him have the information to access his well-hidden bank accounts along with instructions on how he would like the money in those accounts to be used. He'd even considered donating the bulk of the money to his chosen charities and unlike David Walker, since Mark Watton had gone on the run, he'd given the matter and the very real possibility of his own capture a considerable amount of thought. He had a very clear plan of what he would like to happen in this eventuality, and he took steps to ensure his wishes could be carried out should the worst thing happen.

One thing that both men had in common now was they had been caught, and the acute shame and embarrassment they had both brought upon their families. Neither of them was prepared for the pain they'd inflicted on the ones closest to them. Their families were proud of their careers in the RAF and of the fact they were serving their Queen and country. The shame etched onto the faces of their own family members who had turned up in court during their trials was worse to them than ruining their own lives.

DCS Philip Wright from the National Crime Agency received a police commendation for his work in capturing the two men but while the other two known members of the smuggling ring remained at large, the case was still an active investigation; he wanted the other two men caught and caught quickly. The DCS and his team now turned their attention to tracking down Mark Watton and Paul Wilson and bringing them both back to face justice.

An urgent red notice was sent to Interpol to be issued to police forces throughout Europe. DCS Wright would leave no stone unturned in the search for the other two men.

Chapter 25
The Inside Meeting

Flight Sergeant George Stewart was described as a 'professional enabler' to organised crime by Inspector Paul Beard of the National Crime Agency, whilst giving evidence against him. Inspector Beard told the court that organised crime groups rely on professional enablers like George Stewart to supply cocaine across the UK. He went on to describe how George had abused his position in the RAF to contribute to the smuggling operation and supply cocaine to organised crime. He said that George Stewart was an important link in the chain and disrupting activities of men such as him was a key priority for the National Crime Agency.

After sentencing and his dishonourable discharge from the RAF, he was sent to HMP Walton Prison in Liverpool to begin his fourteen-year sentence. George regarded his sentence to be quite lenient, as he was expecting to get at least eighteen years, the same as David Walker had received; he assumed this because the police had not recovered any of the money he'd personally made from the operation.

There were three main reasons why he'd received' a lighter sentence than David Walker. The first was his rank. The trial judge, the Honourable Mr Justice Houseman, wrongly assumed that Squadron Leader Walker, being the commissioned officer and senior-ranking officer, was the leader and the brains behind the smuggling operation and that he'd been the man who had originally thought of the idea and had then recruited George Stewart to help him with his plan. As the instigator and leader of the drug-smuggling ring, it was assumed that Walker received the lion's share of the proceeds and the judge sentenced him accordingly.

Secondly, George's barrister had successfully argued that after serving a tour in an active war zone during the Afghanistan campaign, where he'd served with distinction and had been decorated for his actions. He was now suffering from adjustment disorder. This little-known condition had affected Flight Sergeant Stewart's mental health, to the point where he was easily recruited into the smuggling ring against his better judgement.

Thirdly — and the reason George knew to be the true reason for him not receiving a substantially longer sentence — was that David Walker had kept his mouth shut under police questioning. David was also his friend, and he hadn't disclosed a single piece of information to the police which could have been used to increase George's guilt or to help with the search for Mark Watton or Paul Wilson. Neither man had said anything during questioning and while it was expected that none of the four men would talk under police questioning, it was good to know that both David Walker and he had stuck to this agreement.

George Stewart's barrister had even made Inspector Beard tell the court that it had become known during the police financial investigation that a small percentage of the proceeds had been donated by the men involved, to the RAF Benevolent Fund. Although it was debatable that this particular fact had contributed to George Stewart receiving a more lenient sentence, it was not brought up by David Walker's defending counsel and in the eyes of the trial judge, it was a fact that certainly hadn't hurt George Stewart's defence.

It was an absolute certainty that, had the facts of both of the men's involvement become known during the trial, the sentences they received would have been reversed. The resistance to interrogation training that the RAF had given both men had played a part when they were under questioning.

George had only been in prison for a matter of days and while he was settling in and adjusting to his new life at HMP Walton, he was very surprised to meet his old friend Mickey Ryder. Mickey had already served six months of a two-year sentence in Walton. Mickey had received the sentence after being found guilty of supplying cannabis resin. It was a sentence he would serve only twelve months, with remission for good behaviour. The fact he was in prison was unusual, to say the least, and the fact he was in prison for supplying cannabis resin was highly unusual as Mickey had never dealt with or supplied cannabis in his life. It transpired that during one of the regular police raids and searches at one of his properties, the police had found a kilo of cannabis resin which had been unconvincingly 'hidden' under some clothes in the top drawer of a bedroom cupboard. The fact that during the same search the police had missed £20,000 stuffed up the sleeve of one of his shirts in the wardrobe led some to believe the raid may have been staged. Mickey had never served time in prison during his long and highly successful criminal career and this in itself was very unusual for a man in his line of work. The timing of his arrest and the fact that the police found the cannabis so easily made some of Mickey's associates of co-operating as a low-level informant with the police. It was thought this co-operation was what had given him immunity from prosecution although these were just allegations and suspicions which had never been proven.

At the time of his arrest and prison sentence, Mickey had been receiving lots of heat from his fellow criminal associates regarding these suspicions. It was becoming dangerous for a man in is chosen line of work to continue as he was. It could well have been the case that the police were just sick and tired of Mickey evading arrest and prosecution and had decided to plant the cannabis resin during their search.

Whatever the reason for his incarceration and him protesting his innocence, the short stretch he served in prison definitely enhanced Mickey's reputation and standing in his criminal world, and it allowed him to resume his normal money-making activities on his release. HMP Walton was a Category-B prison and prisoners were normally sent there to complete their sentences if they were serving a sentence of ten years or more or they had previously escaped from a lower category prison. The prison did hold some prisoners who were on remand awaiting their trials or were awaiting transfers to other prisons. Mickey was waiting on his imminent transfer from HMP Walton to HMP Wymot, a Category-C open prison to serve his final six months of his sentence. HMP Wymot was a low-security prison where some prisoners were allowed day releases to work back in the general community as part of their rehabilitation before release.

Chapter 26
Cottage Pie for Moussaka

It is very difficult for a person to move rapidly to another country and remain completely hidden; a bank account in the country of your choice is usually a necessity but requires at least two forms of ID. To open a bank account, you need three things. Firstly, money; secondly, ID and thirdly, you need to provide proof of address. Money and proof of address were not going to be a problem for Mark Watton. When he had first entered Northern Cyprus, creating an alias and obtaining a fake ID allowed him to live quietly under the radar, but opening a bank account was going to present a big problem. First, he had to get himself a Turkish national identity card. The Turkish had run Northern Cyprus since they invaded the island in 1974 and ousted the Greek Cypriots who had seized control by staging a coup. If he could get an ID card, it would then allow him to open a bank account and this would enable him to move freely throughout Northern Cyprus, quietly and without fuss. To avoid detection this had to be achieved without drawing any attention to himself, and as a foreigner on the run from the British police and military.

Unknown to him, there had been a recent shift in attitudes towards Britain and the West in general as Turkey wanted to try to become part of the European Union. An extradition treaty did not exist with the UK, because Britain did not want to risk upsetting Greece or Southern Cyprus. The Turkish Cypriot Police, who policed Northern Cyprus, were now prepared to work closely with British law enforcement and give assistance in locating returning known criminals to the UK to face justice.

Ex-RAF Sergeant Mark Watton had cut all contact with his family, friends and colleagues and was unaware that George Stewart and David Walker had been caught, tried and sentenced in his absence. Both men were already in prison and serving their sentences.

'Mark had needed to flee the RAF and get out of the UK quickly when his excessive gambling with his share of the proceeds from the smuggling operation had come to light. He was certain that if he'd remained it would have led to his own rapid arrest and imprisonment. He, like most military men, was a good planner and men like him always had a fall-back position. All four men had already made some preparations in case the operation was compromised and his country of choice, to flee too, was Northern Cyprus. It was not without any preparation or a last-minute thought to go to Cyprus. As he boarded a commercial flight from Birmingham to Larnaca Airport in Southern Cyprus, he wondered to himself if this was the last time he would be on British soil.

Six months prior to him being AWOL and on the run from the police, George Stewart had purchased four new passports from an acquaintance introduced to him by Mickey Ryder. The person who'd sold him the passports worked in the Liverpool Passport Office and these were genuine passports that contained their fake details and photographs. Each member of the smuggling ring had paid £7,000 each to George Stewart to buy a new passport, each of which contained the name of four deceased men. He'd explained to them, at the time of giving each man his new passport, that these passports are fake, and only to be used after they'd left the county. They were bought for ID purposes only and as an insurance policy to be used sparingly.

All UK passports are biometric and although they had all four of the military men's genuine photos on the passports, they also contained other information which could not be faked and may be flagged at a UK airport on an attempted exit.

The information inside the passports, such as the deceased men's fingerprints, their dates of birth and their professions, and entry and exit details of when they had last used them, would not stand up to scrutiny by UK customs officers. Under no circumstance were they to be used to leave the UK, but they would pass for genuine ID documents abroad.

It was a formality for Mark Watton to collect his single case and clear customs at Larnaca Airport using his own genuine passport. His reason for visiting, when asked, was that he was going to visit a friend based at the army base at Protaras and also to have a few much-needed weeks' rest and recuperation in the lively resort of Ayia Napa. This was something he'd done in the past and so he was admitted entry to Cyprus without any problems.

Once out of the airport, he took a taxi to Larnaca Beach. A couple of streets back from the beachfront and out of sight of any people, he transferred his belongings into the new luggage bag that he'd brought with him. He got rid of his original case, dumping it in a refuse bin located at the side of a quiet café, where he ordered a light lunch and a glass of wine. He was going to try to enjoy his new life on the run, whenever he got the opportunity, without attracting too much attention to himself.

He used the café toilet to change into a fresh set of clothes and put the clothes he'd changed out of in the toilet bin. After lunch, he caught another taxi hailed from the taxi rank at the beach promenade and went back to the airport. After arriving back at Larnaca Airport, he used his fake passport to purchase a one-way ticket to Ercan Airport in Northern Cyprus. He had watched the girl on the counter of the Cyprus Airways desk for thirty minutes before he approached her to buy his internal flight ticket to Ercan. Apart from a cursory glance at his fake British passport and after briefly using it to write his fake name of Mr Kevin Fearns on the ticket for his flight, which he'd paid cash for, she handed his passport back along with his ticket without further ado. Although it was a short internal flight, he was still going from South to Northern Cyprus. They were on the same island but ruled by different countries. He still had to pass through an x-ray machine where the customs officer glanced at his passport, but he seemed to be bored and barely paid him any attention. He went to the departure lounge and sat down to await his flight.

He was worried about the Northern Cypriot side that was ruled by the Turks. He wondered if his fake British passport would be accepted, and he would be allowed entry without any stringent checks.

The thirty-two-minute flight from Larnaca to Ercan was uneventful and really quick. He barely had time to get comfy in his seat when it was time to get off again. This was the most dangerous part of his plan, as the Turkish authorities were known to have strict security measures in place. His heart was pounding but he forced himself to look and act calm. As he approached the booth of the customs section, which had many armed and serious-looking officers, he pushed his passport into the small open space of the booth, with the page containing his details and photograph open.

The officer looked at his passport and looked at him and snapped, "Purpose of your visit?"

Mark Watton replied, "A short holiday"."

The officer looked at his details then handed back his passport and simply said, "Enjoy your holiday, Mr Fearns."

His new identity was now Mr Kevin Fearns, a heating engineer from Liverpool and he'd managed to get into Northern Cyprus without any problems at all.

Chapter 27
The Groundwork

Mark Watton aka Mr Kevin Fearns left Ercan Airport and located a taxi driver who spoke poor but understandable English. He negotiated a fee of 250 Turkish lire, which he didn't have but the taxi driver agreed to be paid £30 sterling and for him to be taken on a long 45 km transfer to the quiet harbour village of Bogaz next to the main coastal town of Iskele.

He made a mental note to himself to change some money into Turkish lira as soon as he could. The taxi journey seemed to take an eternity, but it actually took less than an hour—or fifty minutes to be precise, all the time the driver tried to make small talk and asked questions of the usual tourist kind. "Are you here on holiday? How long are you here for? Do you need any tours organised?"

He didn't feel like replying to the driver. Eventually, the taxi driver gave up with the questions, only after he had recommended a small hotel in the village located on the sea front in the village of Bogaz. It was agreed he would be taken there, and he also noted it was pronounced 'Boaz' with the 'g' silent.

He thought to himself that there was a lot to learn quickly in order for him to remain a person of little interest and to blend in here in Northern Cyprus.

They finally arrived at the hotel, it was called The Sea Life Hotel and although Mark Watton suspected the reason for all the questions from the taxi driver was that he was on a commission by the hotel and asked to drop any tourists off there that he'd picked up from the airport and who didn't have a pre-booked place to stay. Mark had agreed to stay at the hotel as he had no intention of staying there for long, maybe a day or two at the most and the farther away from the airport he was driven, the more relaxed Mark Watton now became.

He was less relaxed on arrival at the hotel whilst checking in as Mr Kevin Fearns. He was asked by the lady receptionist for his passport, but he knew this was the standard practice since the hotel had to report all tourist details to the local police. His passport would be returned the following morning, but the procedure still made him a little nervous.

The Sea Life Hotel was the smallest hotel out of only three hotels in the village. It was modern, nicely decorated and newly built. He was given a nice room with a fantastic view of the harbour, and all in all his first night in Northern Cyprus was going to be better than he had expected.

He changed some sterling into Turkish lire and got a very poor exchange rate at the hotel. Afterwards, he went out for a quiet meal to a local fish restaurant and returned to his hotel early after picking up a bottle of red wine to drink alone on his balcony.

The next morning, he woke up in good spirits, with a little bit of a hangover, after finishing off the full bottle of red wine, before going to bed.

He showered got dressed and went down to the reception desk where they returned his passport to him. He left the hotel, forgoing breakfast, to explore his surroundings. He had a lot to do and organise in a short space of time if he was to make his new life work out.

During the short walk down to the harbour front, he noticed a news and magazine section situated in the corner of a small supermarket and he went in to look for an English newspaper to read while having his breakfast in one of the small cafes. There were no English newspapers but there were a couple of Turkish newspapers written in English. These contained mainly Turkish news stories, but they did cover international sport, so he picked one up. He was about to pay for his paper when out of the corner of his eye he noticed a small notice board on the wall and amongst the Turkish messages pinned on the board, there was an English one, which read, *British expat club meets every Monday and Friday at eight p.m. at the Yavas Bar, all welcome!*

Today was Friday and he made a mental note to find the Yavas Bar and see if he could get some useful information; in particular, how to obtain temporary residency would do very nicely for him just now. His cover story was going to be that he was a retired heating engineer who had recently been divorced from his long-term partner; he'd decided to sell up and leave the UK in search of quiet and peaceful life in Northern Cyprus.

He had a local breakfast consisting of grilled halloumi cheese with olives and sliced tomatoes with some bread and a strong coffee, in a small waterfront café. After breakfast, he decided he needed to buy some clothes that fitted the climate and would help him to blend in. He found clothes shop nearby and bought a couple of pairs of shorts, some t-shirts, a lightweight pair of trousers and a pair of sandals.

On his way back to the hotel, he looked in a local estate

agent's window and was surprised to see that the property prices in the area were surprisingly lower than he expected: a detached villa with a private pool could be bought here for under £150,000. First things first, he thought. Now that his name was registered as a visiting tourist with the local police, he was going to take no chances and had already decided to quickly get out of the hotel and find somewhere to rent for a short time. He thought that maybe the expat group he was going to meet that evening would help him with this, as well as giving him some information about how to become a resident.

It was 8.10 p.m. when he walked into the Yavas Bar, it was unusually busy for a bar and while ordering a beer, he noticed a group of people gathered together at a couple of tables in the corner of the bar. The group was made up of six women and three men; all middle-aged and they were speaking English. he had found the British expat club.

He walked over to introduce himself to the nearest person, who was a short man with a reddish face, wearing shorts and in his opinion, a bad flowered shirt.

"Hi, I'm Kev; I'm looking for the expat club?"

The man stood up and with a smile on his round, red face said, "Well, you've found us, Kev. I'm Mike Bowers, the unofficial chairman and general dog's body, but it's just plain Mike to you. Sit yourself down and let me introduce you to the others. This is Kev, everybody!"

The group stopped talking and all eyes turned to look him over. He got the feeling he was being assessed as potential boyfriend material by the ladies in the group and this made him feel uncomfortable, but he smiled as they all individually introduced themselves. The inevitable questions began. The first one was from one of the men. He was a suave sophisticated-looking gent sitting facing him, "How long have you lived here, Kev?"

He already disliked the man, but his reply was, "I haven't been living here yet. I only arrived a few days ago. I've come along tonight to try to get some help with that."

Mike Bowers chipped in. "Well, you've come to the right place, Kev."

He was in the bar for another three hours before agreeing to meet up again on Monday night and in between the bad jokes and the even worse karaoke singing, it had turned out to be an extremely good night for him to get information. He was given the name and address of a decent apartment complex that had apartments for rent. The very next day, Saturday, he had checked himself out of The Sea Life Hotel and negotiated a rented two-bedroom apartment on a short three-month lease, which was very reasonably priced. It turned out to be a lot more complicated than he first thought and to get a temporary residency permit, which only lasted a year and had to be renewed annually. The checks for a permanent residency permit were even more stringent but he thought that the key to solving his problems was money and he still had plenty of that left.

He'd listened intently to how he needed a blood test and a medical from the local medical centre to obtain a medical certificate that would prove he didn't have hepatitis or AIDS. Unfortunately, although he was heterosexual and had no problems himself with accepting gay people as people, gay men were not welcome in Northern Cyprus and were frowned upon by the Turks. In addition to the medical certificate, he also needed to submit an application form for residency along with a copy of the sale papers for any property that had been bought for him to live permanently in along with a copy of his latest bank statement, showing that he'd enough funds to cover his living expenses. All of this had to be submitted and approved by the local police station. Once the police had approved his residency application, it still had to be approved at the main Immigration Department in Lefkosa. After all this had been approved, he was then required to visit the local muhatar. The muhatar was the village head, a kind of mayor, but with a lot more powers than that of a British Mayor. He also had to be paid a fee by any foreigner who wanted to be allowed to live peacefully and undisturbed in Bogaz.

Mark Watton alias Kevin Fearns realised from the very beginning the key to getting all of this red tape and paperwork approved and to be able to live there and be left alone by the authorities and the police was money! He figured officials could be tactfully given a financial incentive along with the required fee's, which would quickly allow him to get this paperwork approved and for him to gain permanent residency. As it turned out he was spot on about how things worked there!

Four months later it had cost him nearly £15,000 in fees and financial incentives, to the local police and the muhatar. During this time, he had his permanent residency papers approved and had also been issued with an identity card, which allowed him to move freely throughout Northern Cyprus, although he had stayed firmly put, not venturing very far at all.

He'd bought a small, detached villa with its own private pool located on a hillside above Bogaz, with mountains to the rear and superb views of the sea and harbour at the front. He'd also bought a small car, a two-year-old Fiat, which he'd paid the equivalent of a new one back in the UK. Prices of cars were very expensive in Cyprus.

As he sipped a glass of local wine and took in the fantastic sea view from his villa balcony, he found himself thinking, *this will have to do, Mark; this will just have to do!*

Chapter 28
The Prison Break

George Stewart had served the first nine months of his fourteen-year sentence in the antiquated, Victorian built HMP Walton Prison, located in Liverpool.

He'd done this without a single protest. Being a military man, he had just got on with serving his time. It would not have made a single difference if he'd have moaned or protested during those nine months and in any case, he found it wasn't too bad. He had plenty of time to read and he was allowed access to the gym and the yard for exercise. He'd initially been helped to settle into prison life during the first two months with the help of Mickey Ryder, who was also incarcerated in HMP Walton; they'd become firm friends as well as past partners in crime. He was sad to see Mickey go when he was transferred to HMP Whymot, an open prison, in preparation for his release. George Stewart was only forty-nine but this still made him one of the older prisoners in HMP Walton and because of his age and coupled with his natural air of authority and calm demeanour, he was made a prison mentor. A prison mentor's job was to calm down and talk to younger prisoners who had on occasion resorted to using extreme violence on the prison officers who were referred to as 'screws' by the prisoners. Others had got themselves involved in violent fights against fellow prisoners. At the other end of the scale were young prisoners who had self-harmed or in extreme cases tried to take their own lives. Some had been put into a cell on their own on what was called 'suicide watch'. There were a variety of reasons why young men acted in this way, such as bullying, missing loved ones or just being caged. All of these reasons were a way of drawing attention to themselves and their plight; it was really a cry for help.

No matter what crimes they had committed they were still just young men, and as a mentor, it was George Stewart's job to listen and talk to these young men, try to calm them down and reassure them. His main job was listening; he should have been called 'prison listener'. When he was first offered the job, he asked for some time to think about it before he accepted it. His reasoning was that it might take his mind off his own problems and even make his own time go a little bit quicker. The job came with him having his own cell and being allowed the privilege of keeping his own personal toaster in his cell. He'd never liked sharing a cell with another prisoner, so it suited him to be a prison mentor.

One particular morning, George Stewart woke in his cell in agony with severe stomach pains; he was admitted to the prison medical centre where he yelped every time the doctor pressed on the lower right side of his abdomen. He also felt extremely nauseous and generally very unwell. The prison doctor diagnosed appendicitis and arrangements were made for him to be immediately transferred to the local Aintree University Hospital for treatment. On arrival at the hospital, his symptoms appeared to be getting worse.

The hospital security guard had been informed of their imminent arrival by a phone call from one of the guards at the prison before they had set off; the hospital guard, along with a doctor and a porter, were waiting at a side entrance of the hospital, which was the agreed meeting point for a prisoner requiring medical treatment. The white prison van pulled up reversed and came to a stop in the loading bay opposite the hospital doors. The back door of the prison van opened revealing George Stewart, handcuffed to the prison officer; he was lying on the long side seat of the prison van, groaning in pain and clutching his lower stomach. He was stretchered off the van with the porter at the rear of the prison officer; he was still handcuffed to him at the front of the stretcher. All the while this was happening, the doctor was protesting and pleading to the prison guard to remove the handcuffs, but his protests were in vain as the guard wouldn't remove them. With the doctor still protesting they transferred him from the stretcher out of the van and onto a hospital gurney, that the porter had waiting for their arrival. With the hospital security guard holding one of the doors open, they quickly pushed him inside of the hospital corridor. All five men made their way down the corridor towards the radiology department where a radiologist was already set up and waiting to take x-rays of his stomach. All the time they pushed him on the hospital gurney, George Stewart kept moaning and groaning that he was in considerable pain.

After quite a long walk and passing through three separate corridors they reached the radiology department, which had a sign on the doors saying 'no unauthorised entry'. Even then, the prison guard was reluctant to remove the handcuffs, but after the doctor explained to the prison guard that an x-ray could not be taken in the presence of any metal and he would be subjecting himself to unnecessary radiation, he finally agreed to remove the handcuffs and George Stewart was pushed into the radiology department, still in pain and moaning out loud. The doctor and the porter followed him in, while the prison guard and hospital guard stayed outside and sat on a bench facing the x-ray department. The doctor explained to both guards that the x-ray procedure would take around fifteen to twenty minutes and under no circumstances must the room be entered when the red light above the door was on for fear of radiation contamination.

Once they had entered the x-ray department, they passed through a second set of doors and into the main x-ray room. The doctor flicked on the switch which illuminated the red light, and he quietly locked the second set of doors behind him, leaving the key in the lock while the porter switched on a small portable tape recording of a man groaning in pain.

In the lead-lined corner booth, the real doctor and the radiologist and a nursing assistant were all securely tied, gagged and bound. The man wearing the doctor's clothes said, "You can get up now, George."

Instantly George Stewart stopped moaning, got off the gurney and said, "I wasn't sure it was going to work. You overdid the pleading for the cuffs to be removed a little too much."

"It was never in doubt, George," was the reply. He continued, "Those screws love to think that they're in charge, I had to make it convincing."

"There's not much time — let's go!"

The x-ray department was conveniently located on the ground floor of the hospital and the three men crawled through a prepared hole in the x-ray department wall and into a small adjacent storeroom. From there, they escaped through a window and across a small flower bed and into the side door of a waiting white transit van. The van drove slowly out of the hospital grounds with the driver calmly presenting the pre-paid parking ticket to raise the barriers. The breakout plan had taken exactly four minutes to execute and had worked perfectly.

Chapter 29
The Hunt

The prison guard and the hospital security guard had waited twenty-two minutes before entering the x-ray department with the red warning light outside the room, still on. When they tried the second set of doors to the x-ray room, they were locked. It was another six minutes before they managed to force entry through the locked doors to be faced with the unbelievable scene of the real doctor and his nurse gagged and tied up. They needed to raise the alarm, but it was too late, the prisoner was long gone.

George Stewart and his accomplices by this time had nearly thirty minutes to make good their escape. Despite a full security operation by Merseyside Police, including roadblocks and a stop & search strategy within a ten-mile radius of the hospital. No trace of them was found; they were long gone.

The white transit van was found burnt out and abandoned. It had been reported stolen a week before the escape. Face recognition on the fake doctor and the porter proved inconclusive due mainly to the grainy images obtained from the hospital's own cameras. Also, the two men appeared to know where the cameras in the hospital were located, as they always looked down when approaching the cameras.

Under police questioning, the hospital security guard told the police he was told to meet the doctor and porter at the side doors to await the delivery of the prisoner. There were so many doctors and nurses working at the hospital, so he didn't find it a bit unusual that he didn't know their faces. It appeared all enquiries to locate and recapture George Stewart were so far drawing a blank.

When news of George Stewart's prison break reached Detective Chief Superintendent Philip Wright of the National Crime Agency, he was absolutely furious. This meant that only one of the known four military men involved in the smuggling ring was now in prison. That man was David Walker, wrongly sentenced to eighteen years for being the ringleader of the smuggling gang and who was now serving his time in the high-security HMP Shotts Prison near Lanarkshire in Scotland. Shotts was a maximum-security prison for long term adult male offenders who were serving sentences of four years or more and since becoming a maximum-security prison it was known for being nearly impossible to escape from.

The National Crime Agency was once again looking for three members of the military smuggling gang.

There had been some progress in the search for Mark Watton, however. His movements had been traced to Larnaca airport in Cyprus. Airport security cameras had shown him leaving the terminal but not re-entering, so it was now assumed he was on the run in Southern Cyprus, or he had crossed the border into Northern Cyprus.

The borders between Southern and Northern Cyprus had become very relaxed since opening in 2004, and only a valid passport was required at any of the three crossing points. There were two crossing points in Lefkosacar, and Nicosia called Ledra Palace and Metehan and one in Famagusta known as the 2.5-mile checkpoint. The 2.5-mile checkpoint and the

Metehan crossing could both be accessed and crossed by car, but the Ledra Palace crossing was for pedestrians only, and as it was assumed that Mark Watton was travelling under his own passport, it was also assumed that he would use the Ledra Palace Crossing to gain entry to Northern Cyprus on foot.

All the crossing points were checked, and it was verified that none had been used by him. All passport numbers were recorded both ways, in and out. For this reason, the National Crime Agency and Cypriot Police Authorities concentrated their initial search for ex-RAF Sergeant Mark Watton in Southern Cyprus.

It had now been seven weeks since Inspector Paul Beard and Sergeant Carl Gleeson of the National Crime Agency had been tasked to find Mark Watton in Southern Cyprus; they had formed a joint operation with the Cypriot Police Authorities and this was called Operation Krymmenos, the English translation was 'Operation Hidden Treasure'.'

Operation Krymmenos started off badly as it was wrongly assumed that Mark Watton had been using his own passport to travel with and to provide his ID; this, coupled with the fact the border crossings had no records of him using his passport to cross to Northern Cyprus, it was not surprising they had drawn a blank as to his whereabouts up to this point.

Interpol had been given his details including his photo ID and they had issued a red notice for Mark Watton. A red notice was an alert to all countries to request and locate and provisionally arrest an individual pending extradition. This too had proven fruitless and although Detective Chief Superintendent Philip Wright realised that in some cases it could take years to track down and bring back criminals and he was starting to become impatient for a result on the capture of Mark Watton. He now had the added problem of re-catching George Stewart and to add further to the pressure, he already felt no significant progress had been made in tracking the whereabouts of Paul Wilson at this time. The whole operation was now manpower intensive and with many of his NCA officers involved with the investigation, he was aware that other serious crimes needed investigation in the UK daily. The agency's resources were already stretched so DCS Wright decided to try to speed things up. To make this happen and to try to get some progress in the search for Mark Watton he would throw the dice one more time: he decided to bring in one of the National Crime Agency's top detectives on the investigation. This detective would be brought in to oversee and take charge of Operation Krymmenos with instructions to quickly catch and bring back Mark Watton to the UK to face justice.

This throw of the dice was to bring in the head of the National Crime Agency's Tactical Intelligence Department, Detective Chief Inspector Gillian Ross.

Gillian Ross had been involved with several high-level investigations including company fraud, cybercrime and drug trafficking. She was a police officer who was known to get quick results and Detective Chief Superintendent Wright needed an officer who would get a fast result in this case. She was immediately seconded from her UK duties to run the small UK police team now based in Southern Cyprus to catch Mark Watton. Working in liaison with the Cypriot police, she was to report directly to the Chief Inspector.

On arrival in Cyprus, she was met by Inspector Beard and after sorting her accommodation out, she was taken to the centre of operations to be brought up to speed. The centre of operations was a small office in Larnaca Police Station. The first progress meeting was in this same office between DCI Ross, Inspector Paul Beard and Sergeant Carl Gleeson and a Cypriot Police Officer seconded to Operation Krymmenos, to help the small British team.

Gill Ross spoke first, "Tell me, Paul, what have you ruled out Mark Watton doing on his arrival in Larnaca?"

Paul Beard looked puzzled and replied, "We've really been concentrating on what he *did* do, not what he didn't do Ma'am"." Gill Ross said nothing as he continued, "We checked the three border crossings into Northern Cyprus; we didn't find his passport number logged at any of the crossings, but we do know he entered Cyprus using his own passport. This ruled out that he had crossed into Northern Cyprus. This means he's got to be here in the South."

Before he could say another word, Gill Ross said, "I take it you've done exhaustive checks?"

He replied, "We have, and they have turned up nothing here."

She replied, "Good"! "Then that's where we will now start this investigation afresh." "We will now assume he's crossed into Northern Cyprus. The search will start now for him there. Is this understood by everyone?" "Good! let's start by getting me the head of the Northern Turkish Cypriot Police on the phone now!"

With that brief but incisive and correct deduction by Gill Ross, Operation Krymmenos now switched to the correct assumption of searching for Mark Watton on the Northern side of Cyprus. This was why she was known to get results; she made decisions quickly and acted on them.

Chapter 30
The Closing Net

Detective Chief Inspector Gillian Ross and her small team were now receiving the full co-operation and assistance of the Turkish Republic and the Northern Cyprus Police in her quest to track down and locate Mark Watton. She was almost certain that he'd crossed the border to try to avoid detection. She needed now needed to work out how he managed to cross the border from the South to the North of Cyprus without his passport name being registered at the crossing points.

The DCI had asked for and was in receipt of the details of a list of all British expats, who had applied for temporary or permanent residency in Northern Cyprus. Since the date Mark Watton was known to have entered Cyprus, it was an incomplete list, which local police stations were supposed to submit every few months to the Immigration Department at Lefkosa. In reality, most police stations did comply with this request, but a few did not bother or sent incomplete lists. It was of little help to the UK police team in tracking Mark Watton.

In many cases, fugitives on the run were only caught when arrested for another crime or involved in an accident. It was to be one of these occasions that would lead to a breakthrough for the police and point them in the direction of Mark Watton's bolthole.

Kev Fearns had agreed to drive one of the ladies he'd met at the expat club in Bogaz, a Mrs Jean Booth, out for a day sightseeing along the coast to Salamis an ancient city which still had some old Roman ruins. Salamis was located just up the coast from Bogaz, about a twenty-five-minute drive. He'd become very friendly with Jean, a good-looking brunette lady who was a divorcee and roughly the same age as him, in her late forties. She had moved to Northern Cyprus a couple of years before him when her marriage broke down after her husband was caught cheating on her. She decided to move to Northern Cyprus using her part of the financial settlement from the divorce for a fresh start.

They both got on really well and had a similar sense of humour and although he was very guarded when she would ask some awkward questions about his life back in the UK or why he had no family pictures in his villa. She had quickly learnt not to broach the subject and their relationship was now at the friends-with-benefits stage, although it was evident, she wanted to take it a step further.

He was giving the idea some serious thought as he liked her, and it also had the further appeal to him that the authorities would not be looking for a couple residing in Northern Cyprus.

He picked Jean up from outside her apartment in Bogaz at the agreed time of ten a.m. in his Fiat 500. They were both looking forward to each other's company and both were in good spirits. He'd cranked up the air conditioning to its maximum setting and they made their way to the coast road, leading to their destination of Salamis. He was glad that they drove on the left-hand side here, although some tourists drove recklessly even without indicating what direction they intended to travel in at all, which meant driving here required the utmost care and attention.

They were about three-quarters of the way through their journey and no more than two miles away from their destination of Salamis and both were in a deep discussion wondering if they would find a nice restaurant for lunch when the accident happened.

As the car passed a junction in the road, one of several on this particular stretch of the coast road, a small truck laden with crates of potatoes pulled out in front of them without warning. The driver of the truck hadn't even looked before turning onto the main road, giving Mark Watton no chance of avoiding a collision. Just a split second before the impact, he'd swerved the car away from the truck which had caused the car to clip the front end of the truck and overturn; it spun three or four times before coming to rest upside down on its crumpled roof with the wheels still turning on the opposite side of the road. Luckily the vehicle coming towards them was some way off and had seen the accident unfold before them. The man put his hazard lights on and came to a stop. He exited his vehicle and went to the badly damaged Fiat to see if he could try to get both passengers out of the vehicle.

Both Mark Watton and his passenger Jean Booth were knocked unconscious by the crash and remained strapped into their seats. The driver of the car coming the other way had stopped and with the driver of the truck, who had caused the accident and who was uninjured, he ran to the Fiat car now lying on its roof. They reached the driver's side first and began frantically pulling at the door frame; the glass in the door window had smashed but the door had become jammed due to the impact. After a few seconds of both men pulling on the jammed door, it jolted open, and they quickly released the seatbelt holding Mark Watton. He fell with a thud onto the roof of the car and both men managed to pull him free of the car. Unbeknown to the two men the car was leaking petrol from the ruptured fuel tank at the rear, and a small pool of petrol had begun to form on the road.

As both men dragged the driver a short distance from the car, intending to go back and free the passenger, the car exploded into a fireball. The flames engulfed the car, blowing both men over in the process of attempting to carry Mark Watton to safety. The explosion and the resulting flames prevented any attempt by the men to try to return to the vehicle to rescue the passenger. Mark Watton appeared badly injured and covered in blood, but he was alive.

The local police attended the accident and were on the scene within minutes realising it was an accident that involved a fatality they immediately called for a traffic unit to come to the scene and take over the investigation. The vehicle still contained Jean Booth's burnt body, which was still in the burnt-out shell of the Fiat car. The wreckage was quickly covered over with tarpaulin by the police, which they had removed from the truck, where it had been used to cover the potato crates.

One of the officers put Mark Watton into the recovery position and stayed with him. The other officer took statements off the badly shaken truck driver and the man from the other car who had stopped to help. They now awaited the ambulance to take the injured and still unconscious driver of the car to the main hospital at Lefkosa. The traffic officers who had arrived on the scene remained calm and one of the officers now started taking photographs of the scene while the other traffic officer went to help the officer attending the driver. As soon as he reached the injured driver his eyes widened. Despite the driver's face being partially covered in blood from a small cut to his forehead sustained in the crash the officer still recognised the man. He was now looking at as the man in the picture of the Interpol Red Notice that he'd seen and been looking at only the day before. He wasn't one hundred per cent sure, but he was sure enough that it was the same man from the picture issued by Interpol that he immediately got on his radio to ask one of his colleagues at the station to attend the accident and to bring the picture from the Interpol Red Notice with him.

He called the other police officers together to inform them of who he thought that the injured drive was. There was no time to reflect on this as the ambulance arrived. It was very unfortunate for Mark Watton that this particular traffic officer had been called to the crash scene and ex-Sergeant Mark Watton alias Kev Fearns was now, in effect, captured.

DCI Gill Ross was immediately informed of his capture. She turned to Inspector Bear and simply said, "We've got him, Paul!" She now had another satisfying phone call to make to the London Offices of The National Crime Agency and to a Detective Chief Inspector Philip Wright.

Chapter 31
Getting Lucky and Staying Caught

When the news of Mark Watton's capture in the Turkish Republic of Northern Cyprus reached DCS Philip Wright, he was elated. He had been getting pressure from the Director-General of the National Crime Agency, Linda Orton, to scale down the investigation and the search for the military men. The Director-General was constantly reminding Philip Wright that it was not his personal crusade to capture and bring these men to justice and that there was a limit to the number of resources that could be utilised on this particular case. Philip Wright respected Linda Orton as she was a good police officer who had joined the police as a constable, and she was now in the agency's top post on merit. He knew she was right as there were plenty of crimes being committed at home, for the agency to investigate.

When the news broke of Mark Watton's capture, it reached him from one of his team members, Gillian Ross, over the telephone, and he was quick to congratulate her. "That's great news Gillian, really good police work."

DCI Gillian Ross was honest enough to realise that the agency had caught a break. "We got lucky, boss, if it wasn't for the accident, God knows how long it would have taken us to catch him."

DCS Wright knew she was right but was feeling in a congratulatory mood as he said, "You're right of course, Gillian, but I think you always knew he was in the North. I'm going to recommend a commendation for all of your hard work."

Gillian Ross took in what DCS Wright was saying for a couple of seconds and said, "Okay, I'm not going to argue with you over that!"

He was about to ask her to make her way to the hospital when she told him she was already there waiting for Mark Watton to regain consciousness before she could officially arrest and caution him.

As it turned out Mark Watton had escaped the crash with relatively minor injuries, unlike his passenger. He'd sustained a fractured wrist and some minor cuts and bruising during the crash making his injuries look much worse but apart from a concussion he was expected to make a complete recovery. The doctor treating him had already been briefed by the local police that he was a known fugitive and after his treatment, it was arranged for him to be moved to a single secure room where an armed guard was posted outside.

As Mark Watton started to become conscious, he slowly opened his eyes and tried to focus on his surroundings. He stared at the white walls of his hospital room; he was aware he was wearing a small plaster cast on his left wrist and he was quickly aware that there were other people in the room with him. He was immediately alarmed by the sight of the armed Turkish Cypriot police officer standing at the bottom left of his hospital bed and a white-coated female doctor who was taking his pulse. In the other corner of his hospital room was a tall slender blonde woman smartly dressed in lightweight civilian clothes. His throat was dry, but he managed to speak "Where's Jean, the woman who was in the car with me?"

The tall blonde woman approached his hospital bed, and he was surprised when she answered his question in perfect Queen's English with a slight London accent, "I'm afraid she didn't make it."

It took a couple of seconds for him to take in what she had just told him.

"What do you mean she didn't make it, is she dead?"

"Yes, I'm sorry, she is," was the woman's reply.

He continued "Was it my fault? He came out of nowhere." The woman said, "Yes, we know, the accident wasn't your fault, Mark." She had just used his Christian name — Mark! The penny dropped as he closed his eyes to take it all in. The woman then charged him. "I am DCI Gillian Ross of the National Crime Agency, and you, Sergeant Mark Watton, are charged with conspiracy to supply and distribute class 'A' drugs through the UK. You do not have to say anything but if you do it may harm your defence..."

At the end of the police caution given by DCI Gillian Ross, former RAF Sergeant Mark Watton said nothing except to murmur under his breath, "How unlucky have I been!"

He just lay there with his eyes closed taking in the enormity of what had just happened to him, the fact he was now caught was hard to swallow but even more overwhelming to him was the news that Jean had died. It was irrelevant to him that the crash wasn't his fault; he just kept thinking that if he hadn't been on the run in Northern Cyprus, Jean would still be alive. It was a very hard fact for him to take in and the more he thought about it, the more emotional he became. He quickly reeled in his emotions as he wasn't going to show any weakness in front of these bastards, it was for when he was alone, he thought to himself.

Sergeant Mark Watton was going to keep his mouth firmly shut under police questioning like the other three men. He would take whatever punishment was coming without complaint. He always knew capture was a distinct possibility, but he couldn't help himself considering what price his involvement with the drug-smuggling ring had now cost. The price had been very high indeed, an innocent woman had lost her life and although he wasn't responsible for or to blame for the accident, it was still his fault that she was in the wrong place at the wrong time and her life had been cut short all because of her involvement with him.

His unblemished RAF record and career now lay in tatters. His Uncle Joey had dodged conscription and he was thought of as the black sheep of his family; in his own eyes, Mark had now well and truly surpassed him in blackening his family name. With his dishonourable discharge, and the shame he had now brought on himself and his family, he found his life to be now truly unbearable. After everything, the death of Jean was his biggest regret, Jean Booth was quickly identified as an expat living in Bogaz and it was through her that the trail led to further information about his now-known alias of Kevin Fearns. Both Jean Booth and Mark Watton (alias Kevin Fearns) were traced back to living in Bogaz, where they discovered his villa containing details of his local bank account. The account eventually led the police to trace his main offshore account in the Bahamas where from time to time he had transferred money into his Cypriot bank account without taking any further precautions.

It was this bank account in the Bahamas that was found to contain 1.6 million pounds, which was the remainder of his cut from the smuggling ring. In a short space of time, the National Crime Agency had obtained a court order which allowed them to seize this money as the proceeds of crime.

The Turkish Republic of Northern Cyprus Police were extremely helpful and co-operative with the National Crime Agency and after three days spent in the hospital under armed guard whilst handcuffed to his bed, Mark Watton was handed over to the NCA to be flown back to London for further questioning and to stand trial.

He was returned to London on a commercial flight from Larnaca where he had entered Cyprus. On the flight to Heathrow, he was handcuffed to Inspector Paul Beard and accompanied by Sergeant Carl Gleeson.

DCI Gillian Ross was given a police commendation on her return, for her work in capturing Mark Watton who refused to reveal anything under further police questioning back in London. The charges of conspiracy to supply and distribute class 'A' drugs by the National Crime Agency were then further added to by the RAF which charged him and found him guilty in his absence of dereliction of duty and desertion. It truly was a complete shit storm that Mark Watton returned to the UK to face. By this time, he was resigned to his fate and didn't really care about the outcome. He was remanded in custody to HMP Belmarsh, a high-security prison, to await his trial at the Old Bailey. On the advice of his defence counsel and in light of the overwhelming evidence that the police and the prosecution had against him, he pleaded guilty on the first day of the trial. His defending counsel had advised him that pleading guilty to avoid a costly trial coupled with his good service record may allow the judge to show him some leniency and this would be reflected in his length of sentence.

During his sentencing speech, the judge called Mark Watton "A despicable man, who had thrown away his exemplary service in the Royal Air Force for nothing more than greed." And as a deterrent to other airmen who contemplated replicating his actions, he sentenced Mark Watton to twenty years in prison, with a recommendation that he serve a minimum of sixteen years before being considered for parole.

DCS Philip Wright, who was in court for the sentencing, was pleased with the outcome and the sentence Mark Watton had received and although he was under pressure to concentrate on other cases, he was acutely aware that George Stewart and Paul Wilson were both still at large and he was determined to track them down. He thought to himself, *"two down and now two to go"!*

For DCS Wright it wasn't just about catching these resourceful men; it was making them stay caught and pay for their crimes.

Chapter 32
Flight of the Flight Sergeant

When the white transit van came to a stop, George Stewart, Mickey Ryder and Tony Powell — another of Mickey's associates — got out of the van and the three men transferred to a silver Volkswagen Passat, which had been parked in a small car park at the rear of a block of shops located just a few miles from the hospital. The driver of the van then drove on to a secluded lane next to Allerton Golf Course in south Liverpool where he exited the van, removed a jerry can from the back and carefully doused the van with petrol.

He paid particular attention to anything in the car that might contain full or partial fingerprints, covering the steering wheel, the seat belt clips, and the door handles inside and out with the petrol. He then tossed the can back into the rear of the van, lit a small piece of rag that was soaked in petrol and threw it into the driver's side.

It went up in flames instantly as he calmly made his exit and walked casually across the adjacent golf course and then off the course premises to his waiting car parked in a quiet side road. As he walked to the car, he heard a loud bang as the flames had reached the jerry can and the van had exploded. He continued walking without a backward glance. It was not the first time this man had carried out this particular procedure.

At the hospital bedside, both men had played their parts

to perfection. Mickey Ryder had played the part of the waiting doctor, complete with a doctor's formal attire of a light-blue long-sleeved Oxford shirt, blue tie, navy blue pants and black Loake shoes complete with a doctor's white coat. Tony Powell had played the part of the waiting porter, who was also in the correct uniform including a lanyard complete with a fake photo ID hung around his neck.

The three men had already arrived at their pre-planned destination and had alighted from the legally registered silver Passat. George Stewart was safely installed in a small house in Widnes. A town located on the outskirts of Liverpool and a distance of fifteen miles from the hospital as the police roadblocks were put into place around a five-mile radius from where they escaped.

They had used the fastest route from the hospital to the M57 and then on to Widnes, carefully keeping to the speed limits. This was the fastest route out of Liverpool and, as in all things George Stewart was involved with, every single detail of the escape was meticulously planned and executed. George and Mickey Ryder had had the best part of three months to plan the escape whilst serving time together at HMP Walton. After lying low at the house in Widnes for over a week, it was now time for the next phase of the plan.

The National Crime Agency, in partnership with The Police Border Force, had already issued details and photographs of George Stewart and were watching for his departure at all the usual air- and seaports. It was decided at the planning stage of the escape that he should be flown out of the country from a small regional airport to France, from where he could make his way to a country of his choice.

He'd already obtained fake papers including a passport,

driver's licence and British Medical Card complete with a new National Insurance Number; these were all real documents but in a fake name of Mr Jack Rushton. They would stand up to a certain amount of scrutiny and documents like these had been used successfully to assist criminals to leave the country on previous occasions.

They decided that in George Stewart's case with his recent prison escape and the fact that National Crime Agency and Border Force were actively engaged in a current operation to recapture him, it was just too risky for him to try to use any of the large UK ports or airports to leave the country.

A week later George Stewart left the small safe house where he'd been taken. He left with the man who played the part of the porter during his escape from the hospital; he was then driven from Widnes to Oban Airport in West Scotland by Tony Powell. Tony was a small, dark-haired man and despite his small stature, he was a mentally strong character and could be relied on to stay cool under pressure. George Stewart liked the man and thought Tony would have made a good NCO given the chance.

In the car the conversation was about the details of the escape plan, Tony spoke in a jovial tone, "You ready George? I wouldn't fancy this flight of yours! This plane's got a lawnmower engine!"

George Stewart just laughed before he replied, "Planes are what joiners use, Tony! "It's aircraft that fly." He remembered hearing himself saying that to trainees in the RAF. That seemed so very long ago now. Oban Airport is a quiet little airport situated on Scotland's West Coast at the beginning of the Highlands. It's run by Argyle and Bute council and only has one commercial airline located there which is the

Hebridean Air Services. They operated a scheduled service flight to the Islands of Colonsay and Islay. a couple of times a week.

George Stewart was driven past the main airport building to a wooden bar gate which led up a short loose-stone road leading to the airport flying school. There he was met by Gary Mackinley, a private pilot and associate of Mickey Ryder. Gary Mackinley was an excellent pilot who'd held a pilot's licence before he was old enough to drive and he'd flown all over the UK and on a couple of occasions he'd made the trip over to France. George Stewart eyed up the small stocky Scotsman. Gary Mackinley spoke, "Mr Rushton, I'm Gary good to meet you. Let's get you out of sight and into the flying school building. Hey?"

George didn't know whether to be happy or angry that the pilot had been told his alias name of Jack Rushton but he just said, "Yes, that's a good idea and it's Jack. Nice to meet you too, Gary."

It was impossible to fly to France from Oban nonstop in a twin-seater Cessna Skycatcher without refuelling stops, so Gary Mackinley had already logged their flight plan to France with stops scheduled for refuelling at Black Hill Airstrip in Northern Ireland, Cotswold Airport in Gloucestershire and then on to their final destination, Brest Bretagne Airport in France.

On arrival at Brest Bretagne Airport, George Stewart (alias Jack Rushton) and Gary Mackinley cleared customs with no problems at all. It was done in a small building in the private flight landing area, by a lone official; he also closed their flight plan and filed their return flight plan for the following morning. The airport official barely glanced at their passports, as it was normal for an overnight stay by people landing on a private flight to return to the UK the following morning.

The two men left the airport and got a taxi to the centre of Brest, where they parted company. Gary Mackinley booked into the Oceania Hotel for an overnight stay and George Stewart went to his arranged meeting at McGuigan's bar at the harbour where he met up with Mickey Ryder. Just two Brits having a quiet drink in a French harbour.

Chapter 33
The Serbian Sailor

In the Bay of Kotor on the Adriatic Sea, a small cutter sailed slowly away from the shore. On reaching a distance of a couple of miles out to sea, she suddenly tacked and started to gather speed as the mistral winds caught hold filling her headsails and bowsprit. The sailing boat raced back towards the land, dancing on the water, and the man at the helm, Andrej Petrovic, had a huge smile on his face and seemed to be enjoying himself immensely.

Andrej Petrovic was the alias that Chief Petty Officer Paul Wilson had chosen and was now living under. He had chosen the name Andrej as it meant 'manly and strong' in Slavic and Petrovic was a common surname; it was the equivalent of Smith or Jones in English.

On his arrival in Montenegro, he'd stayed one night in the coastal town of Budva and while there, he'd got friendly and made some discreet enquiries with an English-speaking barman on how residency could be obtained as a foreigner in Montenegro. He had been taken aback when asked directly by the barman if he wanted a legal way to stay or an illegal way to stay.

He responded by saying, "Just out of curiosity how could an illegal way of residency be obtained?"

The answer the barman gave him surprised him. He was

told that either way it would only be a question of money. The legal way was cheaper of course, but it was all a question of money. After Paul had bought plenty of drinks for the barman and himself, the barman gave him the name of his uncle and the address of the business his uncle ran. The man was an English-speaking lawyer in Herceg Novi. The lawyer's name was Gajin Repic of Gojcaj law firm and Paul Wilson was told to say that Gajin's nephew, Radovan, had sent him. Although sceptical, and under the guise of enquiring about legal immigration, Paul had visited Gajin Repic at his offices in Herceg Novi. He had been expected; it really was all about the money. Gajin Repic was now his legally appointed lawyer who handled all of his legal affairs. It had cost him 450,000 euros to gain a permanent residency permit to live in Montenegro; this included a 100,000-euro donation for the development of local poor communities and a total investment of 250,000 euros to buy his house and business premises and a 50,000-euro payoff to Gajin Repic to get all the required paperwork in his new name of Andrej Petrovic. This final payment was an insurance policy for the lawyer, but Paul knew the man would keep his mouth shut as in the Montenegro legal system, appointed lawyers were not allowed to testify against their own clients. The penalties for the lawyer for falsely obtaining immigration papers for him were equally severe as for the person for whom the papers were obtained, and it would usually result in a prison sentence for both parties if caught falsifying papers

Now with his papers all in order, Paul was slowly achieving his goal of blending into his new life and surroundings. As more time passed, he was slowly becoming accepted as one of the locals. He was using the cover story that his parents were both born in the old Yugoslavian capital of Belgrade before Yugoslavia had split into two separate warring republics. His story was that his parents had left and taken him to England as a small child in search of a better life for them all. He'd returned to semi-retire in Montenegro and the town of Tivat in particular, as it was ideal for his part-time sail making business.

He had made it known that he didn't need to work as he'd run a successful sail making business in Torquay and had acquired enough money from running this to allow him a comfortable retirement. However, he told whoever asked that he loved being a sailmaker and could not give his love of sail making up completely. This story carried an element of truth as he now certainly didn't need to work to live. It also covered the fact his language skills were poor and the inescapable fact that he had an English accent. His grasp of the Montenegrin language was rapidly improving, thanks to the frequent lessons he was secretly paying for and receiving from an English-speaking tutor in the small town of Becici, thirty kilometres from where he now lived in Tivat. She was being paid above her normal rates to ensure that no questions were asked or required. He had simply told her he was retiring there and needed to be taught to speak the local dialect as quickly as possible, again keeping his explanation close to the truth. Even with his improved language skills he still couldn't lose his Bristol accent.

His sail making business was actually starting to thrive and he had soon built up a small waiting list with some forward orders. He was in the enviable position of having to actually turn work down. Sail making was work he really enjoyed, it kept him busy, but he didn't allow it to take over all of his free time; he made lots of time for him to enjoy himself.

He was enjoying his new life and knew that if he had wanted to, he could have quite easily made a good living from his sail making business. Although he had more money than he could possibly need, he found himself at times regretting the path he'd chosen and just like the other three, he wished he'd never got involved with the smuggling and finished his time in the Royal Navy. He would still have been able to come to this beautiful country and live here, but maybe not live as well as he was now, but it would have been a life without the moral soul-searching regret he was having to now live with. Whenever he got these thoughts, which were too often for his liking, he quickly forced these thoughts to the dark recesses of his mind and tried to think positively as he couldn't change anything now.

He'd become very friendly with a local single woman, who ran a small bakery in the town. They occasionally stayed at each other's homes, and she was also helping him to practise and learn the Montenegrin language. All in all, he had settled into his new life very nicely indeed.

Chapter 34
The Onward Journey

George Stewart was now using a passport in the name of Jack Rushton while he was staying in Brest. The passport was in an alias name and had been bought from a man who worked in an official capacity at the Liverpool passport office. This meant it was entered into the system as a genuine passport, even though it was in the name of a deceased man. This would allow him to pass through manual passport booths or the biometric gates at the airports without raising a red flag to the customs officials. All four men were told at the time of the issue of their new passports, to use them only when absolutely necessary. This passport would allow him to continue his travels to his chosen destination and would act as his form of identification once there. Every time a false passport was used, it triggered a chance that the computer would not match it with a living person, and this would put the user at risk of detection.

He stayed in the town of Brest in France for four days, staying two nights in two hotels. While there, he used this time to think through his next step and, more importantly, his next destination whilst on the run.

After four days of thinking about what his next move was going to be, he finally came to a decision about the country he would move to next. It was a decision which, when it came to him, surprised even himself.

For the first time since all of his troubles and since he'd dreamt up this whole sorry smuggling operation, he saw with real clarity what he must do next. Ultimately this whole situation, the drug smuggling and now with his friends losing their military careers and good service records and languishing in prison, he knew that it was his entire fault. It was true they all knew what they were getting involved in and they all wanted the money, but he'd been the one who had persuaded them to give up their unblemished and distinguished military careers and ended up disgracing them and their families. There was just no amount of money that could make up for that and he now needed to do the right thing for once in his life.

He had made the decision that the next country he was going to move to would be the UK. He was going back!

He wasn't just going back to the UK for a quiet life of anonymity; he was going back for a totally different reason altogether.

George Stewart was going to utilise all of his military training, his planning ability and his newfound criminal friends along with his share of the money to attempt to break the others out of prison!

He decided that the best way for him to get himself back in the UK was the little-known route of entering through the Republic of Ireland as customs checks were less stringent there than the mainland UK. If he could clear customs there, he could then travel through the non-existent border to Northern Ireland and catch a ferry to Scotland. He knew that British Nationals did not need to show passports to travel from Northern Ireland to Scotland. The trickiest part of his plan was entering the Republic of Ireland from France.

His journey back to the UK started by him taking a four-hour train ride from Brest to Gare Du Nord station in Paris. From there, he transferred to the shuttle train station and took a further 15 km train ride to Orly Airport, where he paid cash at the Transavia flight desk using the passport in the name of Jack Rushton.

It was a direct flight that lasted two hours and fifty minutes from Paris to Dublin; George Stewart was not looking forward to the end of his flight as he knew this destination was going to be the hardest point to pass through out of the whole of his planned journey back. On arrival at Dublin Airport, George Stewart needed not have worried about clearing customs as the civilian customs officer in the passport booth didn't even look at his passport, he just waved him on while reading an article from *The Independent* newspaper on the monitor next to him. George travelled by coach to Belfast where he made his way to the ferry terminal and booked himself on the two hour and forty-five-minute Stena Line ferry crossing from Belfast to Glasgow. He could have boarded a direct sailing to Liverpool from Belfast but given his circumstances, he quickly ruled this route out as being too risky as he'd already been told the police were concentrating their search for him there.

As George Stewart stepped back on the shores of the UK, it took all of his mental strength not to fall to his knees and kiss the ground. Instead, he left Glasgow ferry terminal and made his way to the city centre where, after buying two pay-as-you-go mobile phones, he booked himself into a decent hotel. His plan was to order himself some food using room service and get a shower after his nightmare marathon journey. He realised it wasn't just the journey that had wiped him out; it was the mental strain of having all his senses heightened while travelling as a fugitive. As he lay on the hotel bed waiting for room service to deliver his food, he suddenly realised he hadn't slept for two days, and his body was running on empty. He badly needed to sleep.

Paul Wilson aka Andrej Petrovic had settled in well to his new life in Montenegro; his sail making business was now thriving to the point of him actually having to refuse work from members of the local sailing club. He'd built himself a reputation amongst the local sailing community of being a first-class sailmaker whose prices were reasonable and of being a man with high standards of quality workmanship.

He'd even employed a local lad called Yury Spirin to help him with his business. Yury was seventeen and a big, strapping lad who had hung around the harbour in Tivat asking if he could help virtually every day. In the end, Paul had relented at first letting him go on small errands but eventually letting him help full-time with the business. It was good for him to have a second pair of hands to help move and fold the large sails he'd made. He taught Yury how to do sail repairs while he concentrated on making the new sets of sails. His young assistant did the sail repair work carefully watched over by him.

His sail making business was located in Tivat Harbour; his workshop was a red-tiled old brick building within metres of the harbour itself. It had an archway entrance with two large arched wooden doors which were usually kept open, giving him a panoramic view of the harbour and the moored sailboats. He'd made the workshop brighter by the extra couple of roof windows he'd installed himself to improve the light and in addition, he'd built a small office at the rear with a large window looking straight onto the workshop. It was here in this little office that he did all his legitimate paperwork as well as preparing his customer invoices which he paid profit tax on; these were passed on to his lawyer to file and pay the tax on time. He had come too far in his new life to be caught through non-payment of business taxes.

His relationship with the local baker, Ljiljana Delic, had moved on to the next level and she was now living with him in his villa. Andrej had improved his Montenegrin language skills dramatically thanks to his secret language lessons and he was managing to speak in Montenegrin quite well but still with a pronounced English accent which was evident to the locals' ears. He was able to hold his own during a conversation with the local people. It had helped he was able to hone his language skills with Ljiljana and Yury daily. The explanation of his family history of his parents leaving there for a better life in the UK and him now returning to his roots after his parents had passed away seemed to have been generally accepted by the local community. The local people had stopped asking him awkward questions.

He was now the proud owner of a beautiful private villa which he'd furnished in the local style. It had its own swimming pool and was situated on the side of a mountain overlooking the harbour,'. He owned his own car for which he now possessed an official driving licence in his new name.

The one possession he was most proud of was his 32-ft sailing cutter which he called *'Slobodan Duh'* which translated from Montenegrin into English meant *'Free Spirit'*. This was the one thing that gave him the most pleasure. He'd lovingly maintained and polished her stainless-steel metalwork, so the sun glinted off her. He'd made and rigged her out with a completely new set of the finest sails. He had *'Slobodan Duh'* moored directly in front of his workshop and he loved sailing her at every opportunity he got. With his woman by his side, he was an extremely contented man. Life was good for Paul Wilson aka Andrej Petrovic; in fact, it was better than good.

It was a hot sunny day in his workshop and while Andrej and Yury folded a new set of sails in readiness for fitting them the following day, Ljiljana sat on a chair by the two open wooden doors reading a book while the rising sea breeze cooled her off. She had finished her early morning shift at the bakery and was hoping to persuade Andrej to take her on an afternoon drive and have a picnic up in the mountains. She didn't notice the grey-haired man as he approached the workshop unit.

He startled her by asking, "Is this Andrej Petrovic's the sailmaker's workshop?"

She jumped in the chair at the sound of his voice. In front of her was standing a casually dressed grey-haired man in his late forties and wearing a plain white short-sleeved shirt and blue linen long shorts with brown deck shoes.

"Yes, it is; sorry you startled me then. He's through there," she answered, pointing through to the office at the rear of the workshop.

The man looked at her apologetically and said, "I'm very sorry to have made you jump." Smiling at her, he walked through to the rear office. He opened the door of the office and stepped inside to see Andrej, who was sitting at his desk and going through a list of measurements. "Mr Petrovic?" he asked, holding out his hand to be shaken, "I'm told you're a very fine sailmaker."

"I do my best," was Andrej's reply, "what can I do for you? Would you care to sit down?" Andrej indicated the small

213

chair at the side of his desk. The grey-haired man accepted the invitation and sat down.

"Your Serbian is really good for a foreigner."

Andrej was used to hearing this from most of his customers and just said, "Thank you." He was used to people calling the language Montenegrin.

"What can I do for your Mr…?" Andrej let the question linger.

Ignoring the question, the grey-haired gentleman said, "I would like you to make me a complete set of sails for my yacht, Mr Petrovic." He went on "I don't have much time, but I will pay above the normal rate for your services."

Andrej looked at him and said, "I'm sorry, I have more work than I can handle already. If you would like to leave me your details, I can put you on our waiting list."

The man's response was, "Yes I was told you are kept really busy, perhaps you may get a cancellation and reconsider fitting me in, Andrej."

With that, he threw a business card face down onto the table, stood up and left saying goodbye to Ljiljana on the way out of the workshop.

Andrej picked up the card, turned it over to read it and the colour started draining from his face. The card was in the name of Slavko Miljic, Deputy Police Director, Head of The Herceg Novi Regional Police Unit Tel: 03820 410 500 email: slavmm@state.gov.

Chapter 35
Free and Gratis

The very next day, Andrej called the telephone number of the business card. The phone rang a couple of times before it was answered. "Director Miljic."

"Hello, Director Miljic, it's Andrej Petrovic the sailmaker." "Hello, Andrej, nice to hear from you so soon," was the Director's response. "What can I do for you Mr...? I mean Andrej." The deputy director was toying with him at this point.

"It appears I can fit you in sooner than I thought, due to a recent cancellation," was Andrej's reply.

The Police Director was gloating now "I'm so glad to hear this Andrej—you don't mind me calling you Andrej, do you?" "No, not at all, Director," Andrej replied.

"Good. I'll expect you at the marina at two p.m. today to take the measurements, and my yacht is called *Pobjeci*."

The receiver went dead, and Andrej replaced the phone and just sat in his office chair deep in thought.

I've got no choice but to see this through, he reasoned to himself. He hoped to God that this was the real name of the Deputy Police Director Miljic's yacht as *Pobjeci* meant *'escape'* in Montenegrin.

At two p.m., Andrej met the Police Director at the marina as arranged. Andrej was taken on a tender by Miljic a short distance out into the marina where the police director's yacht was moored. As they approached the yacht, he was very relieved to see the name on the side: *"Pobjeci"*, this made him relax a little but he still felt the urgent need to *'pobjeci'* or 'escape' from this uncomfortable situation himself and he was very anxious to quickly complete the job of taking the measurements he needed to make the sails and return to his workshop away from the police director as quickly as was possible.

The police director said very little as Andrej took his required measurements, he just sat there watching him like a hawk It was only when the tender was sailing back to the harbour wall that he finally spoke, "I will expect you to drop everything and work on my sails immediately, Andrej."

"Of course I will, Director," was the reply from Andrej. It suited him to get the sails made and fitted as fast as he could and be clear of this policeman who made him feel very uncomfortable each time they met.

As the inspector dropped Andrej off, he spoke again, "Ring me as soon as the sails are ready for fitting and Andrej, don't let me down; I want these sails done quickly, do you understand?"

"Absolutely, Director," he replied. As he walked away from the harbour, he was left in no doubt that he was now in a very perilous position.

Even now with his extensive experience as a sailmaker it normally took a week for Andrej Petrovic aka Paul Wilson to make a full set of high-quality sails. It took him only four days working long hours to complete Deputy Police Director Miljic's sails. He made them from premium woven Dacron, and he machine stitched, and hand-finished them to perfection.

He was a very nervous man while working for this high-ranking local policeman but he felt he had integrated well into the local community, having opened his business and learnt the language. It had cost him a lot of money in bribes, mostly paid out through his solicitor Gajin Repic, but he now had all the legal paperwork required to be there. This gave him some confidence that his identity change and story would now hold up to scrutiny. His appearance had changed a lot as he was a lot fitter and thinner since he'd gone on the run. He'd changed his diet to eating lots of fish and vegetables and this was the main reason for him losing over a stone in weight. He'd shaved off his beard and moustache long ago and this, coupled with his longish hair, meant he was unrecognisable as the man who had first come to Tivat.

He was still nervous about making the phone call to Miljic to tell him the sails were now ready for fitting. He gave the matter some serious thought before he made the phone call: what to charge him for the sails or should he not charge him at all? The sails were the best quality that money could buy, and it had taken all of his skills as a sailmaker and a considerable amount of time and hard work to produce them. Charging his normal rate for the work, although reasonable, would not be wise in this particular instance. He also considered that charging Miljic too little or even giving the sails to him free of charge, would be too risky and this would draw suspicion from the Director of Police.

He picked up the phone and dialled the number. "Hello, Director Miljic."

"Hello, it's Andrej, your sails are now ready for fitting." The Police Director seemed pleased. "That's great Andrej, can you fit them tomorrow?"

Andrej was about to suggest the very same thing as he wanted this job over and done with as quickly as possible. "Yes, me and my assistant Yury will meet you at the marina at eight a.m. if that's okay with you, Director?"

The response was "Let's make it seven a.m., so I will see you there, Andrej." He ended the call.

Why the big hurry from the police director, Andrej thought to himself? *Miljic is possibly one of the most ignorant men I have ever met.* He couldn't wait for this job to be over and then he could be shot of this man for good.

Director Miljic was waiting at the marina gate leading to the wooden walkway where his yacht was moored. Andrej and Yury arrived at exactly seven a.m. pushing a wheeled sailing trolley truck that contained the new set of sails.

It took them both a full day working flat out to replace the old sails with the new ones. The *'Probjeci'* looked an absolute picture when she was finished. Deputy Police Director Miljic was absolutely delighted with the end results, so much so that he invited Andrej out for a celebratory meal at The Konoba Mala Barka — the best local fish restaurant in Tivat — that evening. He suggested they could discuss payment over the meal for Andrej's first-class work and the reservation had been made for seven. It was an invitation made by the police director in a tone and a manner that Andrej could not refuse.

At seven p.m. exactly, a smartly dressed Andrej walked into the extremely busy restaurant. He was shown to a table where Police Director Miljic was already sitting sipping a pre-dinner aperitif.

A nervous Andrej approached the table and said, "Good evening, Director."

"There you are Andrej, sit yourself down." As Andrej sat

facing the Director, he noticed the table was set for four. As he took his seat, he asked, "Are you expecting anyone else?" Miljic looked at him and said, "I hope you don't mind Andrej, I've invited two friends to join us, and they should be here any minute now. Oh yes, here they are." A tall dark-haired man accompanied by a smartly dressed slim blonde-haired lady, both sat down at the table. Miljic said, "Let me introduce you to Detective Chief Inspector Gillian Ross and Inspector Paul Beard of the National Crime Agency. Please don't make a scene as the whole restaurant is surrounded."

Gillian Ross said, "Chief Petty Officer Paul Wilson, also known as Andrej Petrovic, you're under arrest!" She started to caution him as Inspector Beard handcuffed him.

Paul Wilson looked at Miljic and said, "How long have you known?"

Miljic replied, "From the moment I first saw you."

Paul Wilson just shook his head and said, "Now I understand the 'hurry'."

He was led out of the restaurant to the waiting police car outside. The very same day his lawyer Gajin Repic had also been arrested at his offices in Herceg Novi on charges of fraud, bribery and corruption. All the paperwork of Andrej Petrovic had been investigated by the police.

It turned out that Deputy Director Slavko Miljic had seen Paul Wilson's details on an Interpol Red Notice six months earlier. He already had a report from the local police in Tivat that the sailmaker resembled this man. They had also seen the red notice from Interpol. The assistant director had a particular talent for recognising faces, even thin, beardless faces especially of a fugitive on the run. His arrest and detection rates had allowed him to elevate himself quickly through the police ranks. Paul Wilson wasn't the first fugitive who had been caught trying to hide in Montenegro.

After hearing Paul Wilson's story of him returning home after his parents had passed away and that they had supposedly been born in Montenegro and emigrated to the UK, the police director has already ordered a full investigation. After finding no evidence of his parents' birth in Montenegro and checking Andrej Petrovic's papers, he knew they had their man. Paul Wilson had been under police surveillance for a week before the director had walked into his workshop and heard his accent. While at the workshop it occurred to him that he might as well utilise this man's talents while all the police suspicions were confirmed and quickly before they made the arrest.

Relations with the UK police and the international police communities had improved dramatically, and the Montenegrin police were only too happy to assists with Paul Wilson's arrest and transfer back to the UK. His arrest would do no harm to Deputy Director Slavko Miljic's career; in fact, he would probably now be made a full director because of it. And an added bonus was that he got his new high-class yacht sails "free and gratis." It was a win-win situation for him.

Chapter 36
The Reunion

It was a surprise when a postcard was delivered to Mark Watton at Belmarsh Prison. The front on the postcard had a picture of the Eastgate Arch on it, in Chester, the place where he was supposed to call a meeting. He knew at once it was from either George Stewart or Paul Wilson. It couldn't be off David Walker as he was still incarcerated at Shotts Prison in Scotland. The written message in ballpoint pen simply said, *Hi Mark, thinking of you, Love Stewy*. This confirmed to him that the card was from George Stewart aka Stewy as it was what Mark would call him on some occasions in a playful way. Although contact had now been made by George, it was still not totally clear as to exactly what message he was sending or what the card actually meant. At the time of reading the card, Mark expected George to be at an exotic location lying low, not in Britain and certainly not in Chester!

George Stewart decided he needed a base to operate from, a place where he would not look or sound out of place. He decided to rent a duplex apartment in a converted chapel in Frodsham. Frodsham is a small quiet Cheshire village located on the outskirts of Merseyside and near to Chester. The apartment had its own private, secluded entrance with parking to the rear and it was only a fifteen-minute drive over The River Mersey Gateway Bridge to Widnes and neighbouring

Liverpool. It was from this base that he would direct his prison breakout operations. The prison breaks were going to be planned with military precision and careful planning, with nothing being left to chance. He'd already purchased a small unobtrusive Ford Fiesta and his next task was to contact Mickey Ryder and Tony Powell.

While George Stewart trusted Mickey Ryder now implicitly — and especially after Mickey had already done for him, making the two men firm friends — he still had to be extremely careful when making contact as he knew Mickey would already be on the police radar. For this reason, he decided to make contact with Tony Powell first and then contact Mickey through him.

Tony Powell was a difficult man to track down. It took just over a week before George Stewart managed to get hold of him. All he'd had to go on was he knew he lived in Allerton, a suburban area of South Liverpool. He started by looking in the electoral register and the Liverpool phone book, but this proved fruitless, so he started to visit the local pubs in Allerton, one a night.

It was while George Stewart was nursing a pint, sitting out of the way in the corner of one of these pubs while people watching and waiting, that Tony Powell walked into The Heath Hotel. Tony was just out to have a quiet pint with a mate and stood at the end of the bar after getting served. George Stewart waited until Tony went to the toilet before following him in and while standing next to him at the urinal, he said, "Hello Tony!"

It's funny that when a man stands next to another man in a urinal, they never look at each other nor usually speak for obvious reasons. Tony Powell got a big shock when he

222

suddenly realised who was standing next to him and talking. So much so that in one movement he jerked up and stopped relieving himself. He quickly zipped up his trousers spraying a small amount of urine on his trousers.

"Fucking hell, George! You've just made me piss myself! What are you doing here?"

A smiling George Stewart replied, "I'll explain when you're dryer, Tony. Finish your pint with your mate and then make your excuses to leave. I will meet up with you in The Allerton Hotel in thirty minutes. Come on your own."

Thirty-five minutes later the two men sat at a table in The Allerton Pub and George explained to Tony exactly why he'd come back and what he intended to do.

"I think you're mad, George," was Tony Powell's response. "You were away and free with your money. You could be living a good life abroad. Just being here you are taking a big chance. But breaking someone out of Belmarsh is impossible anyway."

George was already anticipating Tony's objections and he calmly said, "Look Tony what I'm asking you and Mickey to get involved in, is dangerous there's no denying that, but I've made my mind up and I'm going to try to get Mark out, I feel I owe him that."

"To break someone out of Belmarsh is nearly impossible!"

"You are right! And for this reason, I don't intend to break him out of Belmarsh. I intend to break him out of a prison van, on the way to court. I've worked it out down to the very last detail and you know my plans work already, don't you Tony"? "I don't trust just anyone, usually but I do trust you and Mickey, and I will obviously make it all worthwhile for you.

You can make this your last job and retire in relative luxury."

"Yeah, if it works," was Tony's reply.

"Just think it over and here's a burner phone for you and one for Mickey. My burner phone number is programmed into both phones."

After handing Tony the two phones, he got up from the table and left. As he made his way to his car, which he'd parked some distance away from the pub, he thought to himself, *"If Mickey and Tony decide not to help; I can't do this on my own!"* It was all a waiting game now.

The next day, George got a call on the burner phone from Mickey, "George, you mad bastard! I couldn't believe it when Tony told me you were back in the country; how did you manage that?"

George said, "Never mind all that, Mickey; will you help me get Mark out? You know I've already planned it down to the last detail. If you help me do this, it will be the last thing I'll ever ask you to help me with."

There was a short pause before Mickey said "I don't know why I'm actually saying this George, but I'll help you and Tony's in too! I hope this plan of yours is a brilliant one. George, successful or not it's going to cost. Whatever price we decide on, we'll need half of it upfront. Plus, you know it's too dangerous for you to stay in Liverpool, as they are looking for you here!"

George was just glad that both Mickey and Tony were on board; he said, "The money you both get for doing this will set you up for the rest of your lives. You could both try going straight!"

There was muffled laughter to what George had just suggested, Mickey said, "Steady on now Georgie boy; let's not get too carried away."

George quickly gave Mickey the details of where and what time they were going to meet up in Chester the next day and said, "Thanks Mickey you are a good friend, as well as a bad criminal! Now make sure you don't get tagged tomorrow." 'Tagged' was code for being followed by the police.

George knew the address of Mark Watton's sister Paula, who lived in Warrington. He'd met her some time ago when he and Mark had taken her out for a meal and a drink while both men were on weekend leave from the RAF. He intended to travel to Warrington to watch her house and follow her to try to find out where she worked and then intercept and speak to her on her way in to work. He thought there was a slight chance the police still had her under surveillance. It was unlikely since Mark had been caught but they might have somehow linked her with him, and he wasn't going to take any unnecessary chances. His meeting with Mickey in Chester the following day was now his main priority but for his plan to have any chance of working he would need Mark's sister Paula to become involved. She would have to contact Mark by letter and ask him to apply to be temporarily transferred from HMP Belmarsh in London to HMP Risley in Warrington. Mark hadn't had any visitors since he'd been at Belmarsh, which is what he had requested from Paula in his only phone call to home. Although he was ashamed and did not want her to visit him, all prison inmates were entitled to visits from one main family member. If their family lived far away from the prison, as his sister Paula did, the prisoner could save up his visits for six months and then apply for a temporary transfer to a local prison, usually for twenty-eight days. The accumulated visits could be taken during this time. The prisoner would usually be granted this request if there was a place available at the local prison and Mark Watton's closest local prison was HMP Risley in Warrington, where there was usually availability. If he requested a temporary transfer there, there was a very good chance of his request being granted since he hadn't had a single family member visit while he was in HMP Belmarsh. George was already aware from his own time spent in prison that smuggled mobile phones could be bought and were freely available to inmates who could afford to buy them. He was aware of listening technology, developed by the police, that could now be used to listen in on targeted calls made from inmates from inside the confines of the prison walls. For this reason, the request for his transfer had to be framed through a letter to Mark Watton, by his sister, Paula. His sister had found it so strange that he never sent her papers for a visit and wanted Mark to be nearer anyway. To persuade him to do this, and along with his sister's letter, he received another Chester postcard saying, "Looking forward to visiting you soon, Love Stewey!"

The simplicity of George Stewart's plan was what gave it a chance of working, having been in prison or 'banged up' as it was also known. Seeing the level of security and the response time to any threatened breakouts from inside the prison, he had decided that it was virtually impossible to break Mark Watton out of Belmarsh. It was a far easier prospect to try to effect Mark Watton's escape from outside the prison. This would be when he was being transported from the prison in a prison van. There were several places along the route of being transported from Belmarsh to Risley that would allow them to stop the prison van and force the guard to free him before getting away. But first Mark Watton had to get himself transferred to HMP Risley.

Chapter 37
The Breakout

It took George Stewart another two days to make contact with Mark Watton's sister, Paula, after carefully watching Paula's every move, to make sure she wasn't under police surveillance. Paula hesitantly agreed to write to Mark. It was two weeks before he received his sister's request asking him if he could try to get a transfer closer to home. The Prison Governor at HMP Belmarsh was aware that Mark Watton had not received any friends or family visits. The governor decided to grant him a temporary twenty-eight-day transfer to HMP Risley near his hometown of Warrington.

Once his prison transfer had been approved, a date was set for a week later. He was allowed a phone call to tell his sister the good news and how he was looking forward to seeing her, but in reality, if the plan worked out, they both knew they would probably never see each other again. They both knew that the alternative of another fifteen years spent in prison was a much less appealing choice for Mark. George used these weeks productively acquiring the necessary vehicles and equipment for the escape attempt, although he didn't want to use firearms or hurt the van guards escorting the prisoner. He knew that to make this plan work, at least one firearm was necessary; it would need to be brandished and seen. It was more to imply the threat than to actually use the firearms. No guard had ever complied with a polite request. He left Mickey and Tony to discreetly acquire what he needed.

The vehicles were hidden in a couple of rented garages and were all intended to be left at the scene of the escape. Great care was taken to make sure that none of the vehicles could be traced back to them and as well as wearing gloves during any contact with the vehicles, the engine vin numbers were ground off and the number plates were changed.

Nothing was left to chance and all three men were aware that police forensics officers would be carefully searching the vehicles for fingerprints. The biggest headache George had was planning the route out of London. He knew from his own experience that all routes out of London would be carefully monitored by CCTV cameras. A successful escape was just the first step; only a small percentage of prisoners remained free in the first few hours. Most prisoners are normally recaptured close to the scene of their escape and that's usually down to lack of planning. Arrangements had already been made by George for Mark to fly out of the country from Scotland but after the escape, they would go east; the police would not be expecting this.

They would be expecting him to flee towards the northwest, but after the escape, they would go east to Bristol by train. He'd already rented an apartment in Bristol in a leafy residential street just fifteen minutes' walk from Bristol Temple Meads railway station. He'd stocked up with enough provisions to last two men a week. The escape and journey to Bristol was timed to two hours and six minutes by rail. The tickets had been purchased in advance and all four men needed to board the train bound for Bristol at Paddington Station.

George Stewart had planned it all down to the very last

detail, allowing for the extraction and travel time to London Paddington and then on to Bristol Temple Meads station and the fifteen-minute walk to the apartment. He'd also made financial provisions for Mark to use while on the run from his own cut of the smuggling money, but he knew now that if the escape was successful at some stage in the future, they would both need to work, as this was going to be a costly exercise whether it worked or not. George's share of the money was starting to diminish rapidly, but he focused on how much better he would sleep at night if the plan worked and they managed to free Mark; after all, how much clearer would his conscience be?

The four men had arrived in two groups of two within minutes of each other at the rented apartment in Bristol. They were watching the news reports on the television.

"Three men wearing balaclavas about half a mile from Belmarsh Prison carried out an audacious prison escape. The prison van operated by the prison escort firm GeoAmey was transferring Mark Watton a convicted drugs smuggler and ex-Royal Air Force Sergeant from Belmarsh Prison."

A mugshot of Mark Watton was shown on the screen. The coverage cut to an eyewitness who described the event. Mr Robert Davies, a construction worker who was driving near the scene at the time, described the escape: "I saw three masked men in a Volvo drive across the carriageway into the side of the prison van on the opposite carriageway. "I called the police. I could hear the smashing of glass and screaming from inside the van. I saw some men running towards me, so I got out of my car and ran away as fast as I could into the nearby housing estate. I don't mind telling you that I was petrified." The reporter continued, *"The Volvo was found abandoned in*

Newington Street in Central London. Large numbers of police officers were deployed in a bid to recapture the prisoner and his accomplices." Members of the public are asked not to approach these men as they were believed to be armed and dangerous.

A smiling George Stewart turned to the other three men and said, "I sort of enjoyed that! Mark, meet our really good, and now rich, friends Mickey and Tony"!"

They all started laughing but the man laughing the loudest was Mark Watton. He couldn't believe that George had given up everything to break him free.

George went on: "Mickey — you and Tony jump the train back to Liverpool and Tony you're going to pick us up in a week for the journey to Oban." Tony Powell nodded. "I'll stay here with Mark."

Mickey spoke next, "What will you two do for the next week? You can't leave the apartment!" George pointed at Mark and said, "It will take me a week to dye his hair and eyebrows!"

All four men started to laugh again.

Chapter 38
The Long Goodbye

After Mickey and Tony had left the apartment for their return journey back to Liverpool, George Stewart and Mark Watton embraced each other and Mark said, "I really am grateful to you George! You are a true friend, but I can honestly say I don't think I would have done the same for you!"

George smiled as he broke free from the hug. He grabbed a couple of glasses and started pouring them both a large brandy from the bottle he had bought with the week's provisions. They both looked older than their actual ages, with the strain of what had happened evident on both men.

"Listen, Mark, I got you involved in the first place, I just couldn't live with the thought of you languishing in that cell. Paul's still free and I hope it stays that way. I expect you can use this," he handed Mark a glass containing the large shot of brandy. "To David," he said. Both men clinked their glasses and drank the brandy down in one. "Poor bastard's still banged up in Scotland and it's my fault, Mark!"

Mark Watton sat back in his seat as George poured them both their second glass of brandy. "We all knew the risks. You can't free us all, George."

George just looked at him with steely determination and said, "Can't I?"

The week passed without incident and apart from a trip to

an off-licence by George to get another bottle of booze both men remained in the apartment. The apartment was tidy and both men had cleaned every surface of their fingerprints. Tony Powell arrived a week later to drive them to Oban as planned. George had already arranged for the keys to be posted through the letterbox and collected by the letting agency the following day after they had left, as he wanted no contact at all.

Tony loaded the single luggage bag containing George and Mark's toiletries and belongings into the boot of his Audi and the three men started the journey from Bristol to Scotland. They had only travelled a short distance on the A38 northward towards the M5 when George said, "Slight change of plan Tony! You can drop me off in Chester on the way up, then Mark's going on to Oban."

Tony was surprised but didn't say anything; it was only Mark who spoke. "What's going on George? You aren't one for a last-minute change of plans."

George said, "There's one last thing I need to do, but it doesn't involve either of you."

Despite Mark and Tony's protests during the nearly three-hour drive to Chester, George would not change his mind. He had furnished Mark Watton with a new passport and medical card along with details of a bank account in his new name which contained two hundred thousand pounds. If he was careful and lived quietly, it would certainly be enough for a few years on the run.

It was one p.m. when they arrived in Chester to drop George off. He said his goodbyes to Mark, who had an idea just what the last thing was that George had to do, but he said nothing. Both men had a feeling this would be the last time they would ever meet and as Tony and Mark drove off, a final wave from George was returned forlornly by Mark.

George estimated it would be another six hours' drive from Chester before they would reach Oban Airport, where Gary Mackinley would be waiting to fly Mark to France. He'd arranged with Tony for a call on the burner phone when he had dropped Mark off at the airport.

Owing to the amount of driving he knew that he would have to do in a single day — after leaving Liverpool early that morning for the drive to Bristol to collect them both to drive to Oban Airport — Tony had booked himself in for an overnight stay at The Falls of Lora Hotel, which was about a mile away from Oban Airport. He intended to do the return drive to Liverpool the following day. George made his way to Chester Railway Station and took a quick twenty-minute train ride to Frodsham and returned to his rented apartment.

On arrival at Oban Airport, Tony Powell drove the short journey up the driveway past the airport to the flying school entrance gate where Gary Mackinley was waiting. Gary opened the gate as he saw the car approaching. Tony drove through the gateway and parked by the flying school hangar.

Gary Mackinley made no attempt to approach the car and Tony Powell said to Mark Watton, "Something isn't right here."

At that very moment, armed police leapt out from both sides of the hangar and out of the small, wooded area facing the gate. They surrounded the car. "Armed police! Get out of the car now and lie on the ground face down, arms spread with your palms flat," the police shouted. The two men exited the car and did as they were told, lying flat on the ground on either side of the car, with their arms spread. They were handcuffed and searched in that position. The car was searched for weapons, but none were found. Meanwhile, Gary Mackinley was getting handcuffed by the police officers by the gate and led into one of the police cars.

The two men were getting roughly dragged up off the floor by four police officers when a tall thin blonde-haired woman appeared. She spoke in a clear and precise way, with a slight London accent, "I'm Chief Superintendent Gillian Ross, from The National Crime Agency, and you gentlemen are 'nicked'."

As Mark Watton and Tony Powell were led to separate police cars, Inspector Paul Beard spoke to DCI Ross. "Where's George Stewart?"

"I was just thinking the same thing myself," was the reply from the superintendent.

Mark Watton and Tony Powell were both cautioned and taken into police custody. Then they were driven to Oban Police Station to be held and transferred to London for questioning by The National Crime Agency.

An officer from the Tactical Firearms Squad asked DCI Ross, "Shall we wrap the operation up now, Ma'am? And do you want the pilot taken to the station with the others now?" Gill Ross was disappointed that George Stewart hadn't fallen into the trap. She looked at the officer sternly as she said a very firm, "No! I want everyone back into position, including the pilot as I want the trap re-set in case George Stewart may have taken a detour. He may well still turn up here."

George Stewart was really worried when at 7.45 p.m. he still hadn't received the arranged telephone call from Tony Powell to say that Mark had got away to France. By eight p.m. he'd driven from his apartment in Frodsham to the banks of the River Mersey, where he threw his burner phone into the river.

He knew there was something badly amiss as Tony had firm instructions and he knew George was waiting for the call. He'd stressed that it was vital that Tony inform him that Mark had got away safely. He was back in his apartment, and it was now nine p.m. It didn't take this long to drive from Chester to Oban; he'd have to assume that something had gone badly wrong, and his gut feeling was they'd been caught. But how had they been caught, he thought to himself?

Apart from Gary the pilot whom he'd used safely before, it was only Tony, Mark and himself who knew their plan to fly out of the country to France. As the realisation dawned on him, he couldn't bring himself to believe it. He thought to himself that it had to be Mickey! It still wouldn't register in his brain that it could be Mickey Ryder, the same man who had helped him escape, had also been one of the gang who had freed Mark. It was Mickey who had supplied the sawn-off shotgun that had been used during Mark's escape; he was the same man that knew where their hideout was in Bristol.

George just couldn't comprehend it; there had been lots of opportunities for Mickey to turn them over to the police. Why would Mickey have waited until now to turn them in? Mickey would not have known of George's last-minute change of plan; he would have expected them all to be in the same place in Oban for the police to arrest them all. Doing a deal wasn't an option for Mickey as the police had just as much on him as the rest of them, but the only thing he was sure of was that no one, including Mickey Ryder, knew where George was hiding out and since he'd gotten rid of his burner phone there was now no phone or anything else that could be linked and traced back to him. He still wasn't a hundred per cent positive that they'd been caught and hoped that there was another explanation. It was the next day when the news broke that Mark Watton had been recaptured by officers of the National Crime Agency assisted by Police Scotland. This confirmed George's worst fears, and his heart sank. *How bad must Mark be feeling to be out for such a short space of time, before being recaptured*, he thought to himself?

I had to be Mickey, he mused, but the question was 'why'? Mickey would surely get at least the same amount of time as the rest of them irrespective of whether he had cut a deal with the police or not. He still had most of the money from his cut of the smuggling as George hadn't yet transferred Tony or Mickey's agreed fee for helping him break Mark out. It was only a matter of George making a couple of phone calls to the bank abroad with their account numbers and details and then transferring the two hundred thousand pounds for Mark Watton. One thing he was extremely good at now was banking, and in particular, he'd become an expert in preventing the police from tracing the funds.

George still had no idea what incentive the police would have been able to offer Mickey to sell the rest of them out, even if he'd been caught himself. This was because George had no idea that Mickey Ryder, the man he'd completely trusted up to this point was actually a police super grass!

Chapter 39
The Retribution

Everyone who knew Mickey Ryder knew he was a man who'd made a fortune from various unsavoury borderline criminal activities. He'd made a lot of money from mostly legal property deals as well as a middleman and negotiator in criminal gang disputes but not everybody knew that the money he used to fund his property deals, came from drug dealings. Even fewer people knew that for years, Mickey had worked hand in hand with and supplied information to the police, Customs, and Inland Revenue and on occasions MI5 Intelligence Officers. All the time he was working alongside drug trafficking and distribution gangs, who were bringing in and distributing massive amounts of cocaine and cannabis throughout the country.

What no one knew in his inner circle of friends and family was Mickey had become one of the most highly rated criminal informants in the country. A senior officer in the Merseyside Regional Crime Squad called him one of the best — if not *the* best — informant he'd ever worked with. Mickey provided information against some of Britain's most notorious criminals. The strain of leading a double life as both a drug dealer and informant was beginning to show. He'd developed split loyalties and actually liked George Stewart whom he had befriended and been loyal to at the very beginning.

Mickey was becoming messy in his business dealings and was starting to take advantage of his role as a participating informant believing he was immune from prosecution. At the same time, the police encouraged him to get involved with bigger and more dangerous drug deals, giving him immunity in order to extract information from him that would lead to the arrest and convictions of the top drug barons.

Unfortunately for Mickey, he'd not reckoned with Customs and Excise, that they'd had him under surveillance during a particularly large drug deal that went wrong. They refused to treat him leniently because of the deal he'd struck with the police. He'd been charged with offences connected with this deal and he'd been threatened with a thirty-year sentence for his involvement. Senior police officers had spoken to customs on his behalf and had warned him that all bets were off unless he could provide some major arrest and drug seizures for customs. It was around this time that George had got back in touch and asked him to get involved with Mark Watton's prison break. Mickey had seen this as his only way of getting out of his predicament or at least a way of negotiating a substantially reduced sentence. It became clear to him that he'd no choice but to give up George Stewart, Mark Watton and his own friend and criminal associate, Tony Powell. He also gave up Gary Mackinley, the pilot. He obviously didn't know that at the last minute, George Stewart would change his mind and decide not to travel to Oban with the others. Even when he gave the men up to the police, he was still looking at serious prison time, which would be spent in solitary confinement. When the news was leaked of him being a police super grass, there was immediately a three-million-pound bounty put on his head.

Detective Chief Superintendent Philip Wright of the National Crime Agency wasn't sure how he felt after receiving the phone call from Superintendent Ross to tell him what had happened at Oban Airport. He was jubilant that Mark Watton had been recaptured along with another two accomplices, but he felt angry that George Stewart had yet again somehow slipped the trap. This man seemed to have nine lives. George Stewart was still on the run along with Paul Wilson on whom they'd no leads at all. It seemed that the DCS was destined to only ever have two of the four men in custody at any one time.

The agency had used a lot of manpower — not to mention the time and effort put into this case — and, having caught three of the men involved, he thought it was going to be a case of catching the fourth one to put an end to it. After these latest arrests, they were now using more agency resources and spending more time trying to recapture one and find another

The DCS did not want to admit it to himself, but he was grudgingly starting to admire George Stewart. He knew now that he was the mastermind behind the smuggling ring, not David Walker as he originally thought. George's resourcefulness, exceptional abilities and tenacity marked him out as an unusual man, but he was still a drug smuggler and a criminal; nevertheless, a criminal with rare moral qualities.

Philip Wright thought it was a travesty for him to have thrown away his successful military career for money made from smuggling, the same as it was for the other men but to organise and take part himself in executing Mark Watton's escape from prison, while he was on the run, took a degree of courage, however misguided it was. It was also evident to the DCS that he'd have needed to fund the escape himself as the bulk of Mark Watton's share of the drug money had been recovered by the police. Knowing all of this and that George Stewart's cut of the drug-smuggling money meant that he still would have had more than enough for him to live quietly and undetected and also off the radar, it was clear that this was a man who wasn't money motivated. This was another unusual character for a drug smuggler; any other man would have fled without giving the others a second thought, and this spoke volumes about the man he was hunting: an intelligent, cunning, brave and very loyal man. This man was not the usual criminal drug-smuggling sort, who thought only of himself. George was a disciplined military man, who showed a degree of loyalty to his fellow friends. The one overriding thing he was certain of was that George Stewart was a difficult man to catch and keep caught.

As the search for George Stewart and Paul Wilson continued, Mickey Ryder was charged and tried on major drug offences by Customs and Excise, but as a so-called super grass and under the protection of SOCPA, the Serious Crime and Police Act, his sentence of fifteen years was cut by eighty per cent to just three years. This meant that, with remission, he would serve just eighteen months of his sentence.

The police justified this sentence to Customs and Excise as Mickey Ryder continued to supply them with evidence that led to further criminal prosecutions. His only drawback was he would have to serve the full eighteen months of his sentence in solitary confinement. There was still a price of three million pounds on his head and many of his criminal associates wanted him dead. From this point on, his life would now be under serious threat both inside and outside prison.

George Stewart had quietly cleared all traces of himself from his rented apartment in Frodsham in Cheshire for which he had paid three months in advance. He had handed the key back to the estate agents in the village, making the excuse that he was leaving for a work contract to another part of the country. They seemed satisfied with his explanation, although they were a little bit surprised when he declined to leave his bank account details for them to pay his deposit back, saying he would arrange for his brother to collect it in person the following week.

He drove up to Glasgow and caught the boat to Belfast; he then crossed the Irish border to Dublin and caught an Aer Lingus flight from Dublin to Fiumicino Airport in Rome, using his passport in the name of Jack Rushton. He encountered no problems at all at customs and was now safely checked into Caesar's House Boutique Hotel near to the Colosseum in Rome. He'd travelled for five-and-a-half hours since leaving Dublin Airport and needed to rest up.

Chapter 40
A Dish Best Served Cold

Time passed slowly for Mickey Ryder during his eighteen months prison sentence. It wasn't all bad and although he was in solitary confinement on the vulnerable prisoner wing at HMP Wakefield, his single cell contained a small television with a limited selection of channels as well as a radio. He also had an integrated toilet in the cell. He was allowed out of his cell for fifteen minutes in the morning to shower. He was accompanied by a guard to the empty shower block and also for one hour a day to exercise alone in the prison yard, also accompanied by a guard.

He was allowed to wear his own clothes usually consisting of a tracksuit and training shoes or jeans and a casual top. He was allowed to read books from the prison library as well as the occasional day-old newspapers, which he bought from his weekly allowance of fifteen pounds and fifty pence. From this allowance, he could also buy basic items such as shampoo, deodorant, chocolate and biscuits. To buy these items he would fill a 'canteen sheet' in and these would be brought to him by the guards once a week. His only other human contact while serving his sentence at the prison was his twice-monthly one-hour visits by his sister, who drove from Liverpool to Hull to visit him. All in all, he wasn't exactly doing hard time and knowing he would only serve eighteen months, made it very bearable. He looked at it as having a long-overdue rest away from all the outside pressures and he guessed that he was much safer inside the prison with a price on his head than on the outside.

George Stewart boarded the train for the three-hour-and-thirty-five-minute journey from Rome's Termini Railway Station to Milano Centrale Rail Station in Milan. He booked an overnight stay in the Esco Hotel, just a couple of hundred yards walk from Milan Rail Station. The next day he went back to the station and booked himself on the Nightjet overnight sleeper train to Frankfurt and after a casual day in Milan, he boarded the sleeper train to Germany.

He figured this was the best way to travel to Germany as there are no customs checks while travelling by train from Italy to Germany. He got a surprisingly good night's sleep and the next morning he felt refreshed as he continued his onward journey.

He left Frankfurt Hauptbahnhof Rail Station and made his way to Frankfurt Airport where he had booked himself on to a twelve-hour flight to Singapore. He'd managed to get some sleep but upon his arrival at Singapore, he'd a four-hour stopover before catching another two-hour flight to his final destination of Brunei.

He arrived at Bander Seri Begawan Airport and cleared customs using his British Passport in the name of Jack Rushton, as a tourist, without any problems whatsoever. As he left the airport the heat hit him and along with finding a quiet hotel by the waterfront in the centre of town, some new lightweight clothes were high on his list of things to do. He had spent some time researching where he was going to try to make his new life and had decided on Brunei for several reasons: firstly, Brunei had no extradition treaty with the UK. The ruling Sultan did not like outside interference in his affairs. Secondly, Brunei had an ultra-low crime rate and English was widely spoken. Thirdly, it had good medical facilities, a lovely climate and friendly locals. It did have one or two slight drawbacks as it was a Muslim country and no alcohol was allowed to be sold, although tourists were allowed to bring their own alcohol with them when travelling into the country. George wasn't a big drinker, so doing without alcohol wasn't a particular hardship for him. Brunei, although a small nation, was one of the richest countries in the world, thanks to its exports of oil and natural gas. It was situated on the Island of Borneo and surrounded by Malaysia and the South China Sea.

As a tourist, he was allowed entry into Brunei for ninety days using his British Passport but as in most Asian countries, an extended visa could be obtained quite easily from the diplomatic mission, for a fee of course. A permanent residency was another matter but as in all things, he reasoned, that this too could be obtained for a price.

When Mickey Ryder was released from his short time in prison, he remained in hiding, keeping a very low profile at his sister's house in Ormskirk, a district on the outskirts of Liverpool. After several months he started to venture out, even visiting Liverpool's town centre. On one of these occasions, he met one of his old criminal contacts who invited him to go for a drink. What he found out at this accidental meeting was that there was now a territory gang war going on in Merseyside and the men who wanted him eliminated and had put the contract on his head were off the scene. Some had been arrested by the police on information he had supplied, and others had fled to Spain or Holland; this had left a power vacuum within the criminal world. Mickey was delighted to hear this news and could see an opportunity when it presented itself.

Unbelievable as it seemed at the time, and six months on from the chance meeting in Liverpool, Mickey Ryder was back doing business with the competitors of the men he'd helped the police to put in prison. Although some rumours still persisted that he was again passing information on to the police, this time they were untrue. He quickly got back to what he did best, which was making money in his criminal dealings for the men he worked alongside, as well as making large amounts of money for himself.

He was back, with a vengeance! It seemed as though he'd never been away. The rumours about him and the fact he'd survived having a price on his head seemed to be working in his favour and he was left alone for these very reasons. He now seemed to have weathered the storm. He'd hired himself some protection and travelled everywhere accompanied by a massive muscle-bound man, who was an ex-champion kickboxer and a respected hard man, whom no one would mess with.

Whilst coming out of a North Liverpool pub on a sunny afternoon, Mickey Ryder was approached and shot twice by an assassin carrying a handgun and wearing a surgical mask. He was killed instantly. The first shot entered his head and before he'd dropped to the ground, he was shot a second time in the chest. As his killer jumped on a motorbike and sped off, the bodyguard just stood there rooted to the ground, static beside Mickey's lifeless body.

The shooting was investigated by Merseyside Police and

from the statement given by his bodyguard at the scene, Mickey's killer was dressed in dark clothing and had only a few identifying features, the main feature being a small scar above his left eye. He was of medium build and was roughly six feet in height. The police made every effort to locate the assassin, but their investigation proved fruitless. It was assumed it was an ordered hit and the killer had long fled.

The man sitting at the waterfront restaurant table eating his beef rendang was dressed in local acquired light clothing of a pair of thin linen pants and a white long-sleeved cotton shirt, he was also wearing a pair of lightweight brown leather sandals and from his attire, he looked like a local, but it was only when he looked up that it was clear he was a tourist. He had short brown hair and brown eyes with nondescript features. He had a one-inch half-moon-shaped scar above his left eye which he had received as a child. It was the result of a boy firing a stone from a catapult which at the time had caused a deep gash above George's eye. It was thought to be fortunate that the stone had just missed his eye at the time. George Stewart, alias Jack Rushton, had lived with the scar since boyhood and now as a grown man, he hardly noticed it at all.

Some time ago when Detective Chief Superintendent Philip Wright had been grudgingly admiring the make-up of the man he was hunting, George Stewart, he failed to think of another one of his qualities.

George Stewart was cunning, intelligent, brave and extremely loyal, but there was one other trait the DCS was unaware of was that George Stewart was also a very ruthless man.

George was a man who knew that revenge was a dish best served cold!